CHERRINGHAM

A COSY MYSTERY SERIES

THICK AS THIEVES

Neil Richards • Matthew Costello

RED DOG

UK

Published by RED DOG PRESS 2020

Originally published as an eBook edition by Bastei Lübbe AG, Cologne, Germany, 2013.

ISBN 978-1-913331-60-3

www.reddogpress.co.uk

Cherringham is a long-running mystery series set in the Cotswolds. The stories are self-contained, though many will enjoy reading them in order of publication:

Murder on Thames
Mystery at the Manor
Murder by Moonlight
Thick as Thieves
Last Train to London
The Curse of Mabb's Farm
The Body in the Lake
Snowblind
Playing Dead
A Deadly Confession
Blade in the Water
Death on a Summer Night

1.

THE END OF THE RAINBOW

JERRY PRATT GUNNED the engine of the Land Rover and gripped the steering wheel hard as the wheels struggled against the steep muddy slope of Winsham Hill.

"Come on, you beauty!" he shouted as the engine raced and the old wreck slipped and slewed dangerously to one side.

The vehicle lurched forward, tyres at last clawing into the dirt of the farm track as Jerry regained control.

"Jeez, I thought you'd lost it," said Baz, who was sitting in the passenger seat next to him, his hands gripped tightly on the old metal dashboard.

Jerry looked at his old mate and punched him on the arm, laughing.

"Ha! You was well frit Baz, you fat bastard. Mind you don't wet yourself on my front seat!"

He swung the Land Rover round on the gravel strip in front of the long copse of trees which edged the hill, then stopped and turned off the engine.

"Don't know why you don't just use the track off the cricket pitch like any normal bloke," said Baz grumpily.

"Coz I ain't normal, now am I?"

"Too bloody right, you ain't."

Jerry laughed again, pulled out his cigarettes and offered one to Baz, who shook his head.

"Given up, haven't I?" he said glumly. "Abby doesn't like it. What with the new baby."

Jerry rolled his eyes.

"You want to watch it, mate. You're well under her thumb."

"Yeah well, it'll happen to you one day, Jerry. You just wait."

"No chance. I'm a free spirit me!"

Jerry grinned.

Yep, that's me. Free as a bird, he thought.

Poor as a friggin' peasant too.

He lit a cigarette, grabbed his jacket, climbed out of the Land Rover, and looked around. From up here they said you could see five counties—though he never believed it. Just crap made up by the tourist authority, he thought—and anyway so what? What was the point of seeing five counties? They all looked the same. Just fields.

Still—he had to admit. This time of day, it was a nice enough view. Maybe he should make a habit of getting up before eleven…

He turned back to look at the tree line.

Behind the copse (which he knew was stuffed full of nice plump pheasants at the right time of year) was Cherringham cricket pitch. And behind that was Cherringham itself.

Baz was right—that *was* the best way to get onto Winsham Hill. But it wasn't any fun. And also it was a bit… public for Jerry's liking. Didn't matter what you did round Cherringham, always some busybody ready to stick a nose in, complain, find fault.

So he preferred the back way, the quiet way, the less *normal* way round the village.

Anyway—where was a young, red-blooded, good-looking bloke like him supposed to find his thrills these days? Certainly not up at the chicken factory turning roosters inside out for six quid an hour.

One day he'd be rich and famous and he'd build a big mansion up here looking out over the five stupid counties and he'd sit on the deck at the back, smoking dope and having beers with his mates and the people of Cherringham could stuff it.

"I charged the batteries Jerry, because I knew you'd forget," said Baz from the back of the Land Rover, interrupting Jerry's dreams of a golden future.

"And I didn't bother charging them my old mucker, because I knew you would do just that," said Jerry.

Baz held open the back door of the vehicle and offered up the two metal detectors.

"Choose your weapon," he said, climbing out.

Jerry considered. The Mark IV was heavier—but it gave off less background noise. The Expro-Navigator was lighter, but fiddly.

"Give us the Expro, Baz, got a dodgy shoulder this morning," he said.

"Lifting too many pints I s'pose," said Baz. "All right for some."

Baz handed it over and Jerry rested it on one side while he reached in for his boots. He watched as Baz picked up a spade and the other detector and went over to the crest of the hill and stood, hands on hips, staring out across the valley.

"What shall we do—begin at the bottom and work our way up?"

Boots on, Jerry grabbed his equipment, locked up the Land Rover and joined him.

"Nah, we'll start about halfway, I reckon, then work down."

The top of Winsham Hill was rough meadow—and to one side was the track they'd driven up from the valley. Halfway down, the

THICK AS THIEVES

gradient softened and the land was split into fields of differing crops that went all the way down to the Avon Brook—a meandering stream that curved around Cherringham and fed into the Thames.

"You see Low Copse Farm?" said Jerry, pointing down into the valley beyond the stream.

Baz nodded: "Butterworth's place, yeah?"

"That's the one. He reckons this strip of land has been farmed for a couple of thousand years."

"So there might have been old buildings down there?"

"Correct. And tracks, roads. Places where people sit. Have a nap. Drop stuff. Lose stuff. Bury stuff. Hide stuff."

"Treasure!" said Baz.

"Yeah, well, maybe," said Jerry. "If we're lucky."

"You haven't been lucky yet, though have you?"

"No Baz, I haven't. Which is exactly why you're here. You're going to bring me luck, old son."

"And do half the bloody work for you too," said Baz.

Jerry slapped him on the shoulder. Baz was born grumpy and needed constant encouragement, he thought.

"Well, yes. This is true. But in return—you will get half the bloody treasure when we find it."

"*If* we find it," said Baz. "And even then we have to split it with Butterworth."

"It's his farm, Baz. His land."

"Don't seem fair to me—he just sits at home having his tea and we do all the work."

"Well them's the rules."

"Hmm, if you say so," said Baz. "But this is the third Saturday I been out helping you and I'm getting a bit fed up to be honest."

"Three Saturdays and no treasure yet? What is the world coming to?"

"No need to take the piss Jerry, I'm just saying, that's all."

"I know mate," said Jerry, softening. "So let's get started shall we? Sooner we start detecting, sooner we get lucky."

And so Jerry hoisted his spade onto his shoulder, lifted his detector and set off down the hill to find his fortune.

2.

FINDERS KEEPERS

BAZ WIPED THE sweat out of his eyes and straightened up.

Gawd, my back hurts, he thought.

He checked his watch. Five o'clock. Nearly seven hours they'd been working this field. Back and forth they'd gone across the mud, swinging their detectors slowly from side to side, listening out for the tell-tale ping of a find.

They'd started off walking side by side but then Jerry said they should split up and work different sections of the field. Somehow that was supposed to increase their chances, though Baz wasn't quite sure why.

The furrows went up and down the slope and Jerry's logic was that they should go from one side to the other, working against the furrows. He said they'd been lucky it was just ploughed. It was late for Butterworth to be planting maize, but with all the rain they'd had he'd had to wait till the last minute.

Trouble was—all that rain meant the newly ploughed field had turned to mud when they walked it. Baz's boots were clogged and heavy. So from his point of view, it didn't feel lucky at all.

His back hurt. His legs hurt. And his arms hurt from holding the big damn detector that hadn't detected a thing.

Jerry had picked the lightweight detector: no surprise there. Baz knew he was a sneaky bastard, but he never went up against him. You didn't want to fight Jerry—he fought mean and dirty. He was thin as a length of spit and all wiry. He never seemed to eat, all he did was drink, but in a fight Jerry was all muscle.

Like one of those horrible dogs that sink their teeth into you then get all locked and won't let go.

If Jerry was thin—Baz felt fat and slow. He always had been— right the way through school. Obese, they called it now. Same damn difference. Anyway, Abby was just the same as him and she didn't care so why should he?

He leaned on his shovel and looked across the field for Jerry.

At first he couldn't see him—then he spotted him sitting resting against a fence post, smoking. Jerry gave him a wave.

Baz waved back.

Lazy bastard.

He reached into his pocket, pulled out his energy drink and drained it. Last one—empty. Some fine day this was turning out to be. He'd spent seven quid on drinks and snacks, and what had he found so far?

He scraped inside his trouser pocket and pulled out his treasure. One metal button. Two bits of scrap metal. And three shotgun cartridges.

Still, it was nearly over. Just one last square in the corner to do, then they could head home.

He slung his shovel over one shoulder, put his headphones back on, and adjusted the dials on his detector. Then he held it out so the coil was just above the ground, and set off to finish the field.

Not going to do this again. Waste of bleedin' time, he thought.

JERRY WATCHED BAZ going backwards and forwards like a zombie in the far corner of the field, and he felt anxious. It was getting close to six o'clock and at this rate they wouldn't get to the pub till seven. Way too late for him!

And what was it with Baz? Why was he so slow?

Maybe I should get someone else to help, he thought. *Tell Baz he's not up to it.*

Truth was—he had a soft spot for Baz. His wife was a right bully—and Jerry knew that if he didn't get him out of the house for a few hours now and then Baz would just top himself one day.

And—you had to hand it to Baz—he was thorough. Never walked away from a job till it was done.

Jerry ground his cigarette into the mud and headed over to tell Baz to stop.

But he didn't need to. Baz did stop.

Jerry watched as Baz bent down and dug at the ground, then passed the coil over the mud and dug again. Then he got down on his knees and started scrabbling at the dirt with his hands.

Jerry quickened his step.

Baz sat up, took his headphones off and waved to him frantically, suddenly moving fast.

"Jerry! Jerry!"

Jerry didn't need the invitation. He started running and when he reached Baz, the big man was still scraping hard at the topsoil with his spade, flinging great chunks of soil everywhere.

"Whoa, Baz! Stop! Gently, gently, mate!" said Jerry, kneeling down beside him. "You got somethin'? What is it?"

"Got a giant reading, Jerry. *Immense!*"

"Well calm down, calm down now. Could be anything. Bit of old plough. Buried car. Second World War bomb—"

"Bomb? Jeez!"

Baz stood up fast and backed away, dropping his shovel.

"Or it could be something valuable—in which case, we don't want to scratch it, do we?"

He smiled up at Baz who blinked and nodded.

"Yeah, right. Could be valuable…"

Carefully Jerry scraped more soil to one side and felt with his fingers. There was something there all right, something flat, maybe embossed. He tried to lift it—but it was too big, held down by the thick, solid mud and clay which seemed reluctant to release the prize.

Baz kneeled down next to him.

"Like this, Baz," said Jerry, showing him how to push the soil away a handful at a time. "Nice and gentle."

It only took a minute—and then finally the shape of the mysterious object was revealed.

It was circular—a good couple of feet across with a raised edge. And heavy. Jerry tried to lift it up.

"Gawd—have a go at that! It's bleedin' heavy!"

Baz took the other edge and lifted. His eyes widened in surprise.

"Blimey. It's metal. But what is it, Jerry? Is it treasure?"

Jerry took the bottle of water sitting in his jacket pocket and poured it onto the object. The mud flowed away, leaving the surface underneath black with a slight blue tint. He looked closely. There were figures etched onto the metal, people without any clothes on, dancing, playing trumpets, holding spears.

"I don't know, Baz. It might be an old tray. It might be junk. It might be one of them plates you carve a roast on…"

"B-but it might be treasure?"

Jerry looked at Baz, his face lit up like a little kid at Christmas.

"It might be."

THICK AS THIEVES

Though in truth, he didn't think it was. When had he ever got that lucky?

3.

BY THE BOOK

PETE BUTTERWORTH SAT at the old farmhouse kitchen table, his arms folded, waiting. On his shoulder he could feel his wife Becky's hand—warm, reassuring. He looked around the room. There were five of them in the kitchen altogether—but no one had spoken for some minutes.

At the head of the table, peering at the metal plate through a magnifying glass like some kind of Sherlock Holmes, sat Professor Peregrine Cartwright, one-time Head of Roman Archaeology at the University of Oxford. Every now and then he rotated the heavy object and made another entry in a small notebook which sat on the table in front of him.

Sitting in the kitchen chairs across the table from Pete sat Jerry and Baz—'the world's most unlikely treasure hunters' he used to call them.

Until now, perhaps.

They'd traipsed in just as he'd finished milking, bringing a trail of mud into the house and both talking so much he didn't at first have a clue what they were on about.

Then they'd gently up-ended the old sack onto the kitchen table and he and Becky had both stepped back in surprise.

"We reckon it's a historic tea-tray," Baz had said.

"Medieval, probably," Jerry had added.

The object still had clods of mud on it and the darkened metal didn't look promising, but Pete had seen enough farm finds in his time to know this wasn't a tea-tray.

And it certainly wasn't medieval.

While Becky carefully rinsed it off in the big old kitchen sink, then placed it on newspapers on the table, Pete had explained to the two lads the complicated formal process of recording archaeological finds.

The authorities had to be informed immediately and if that didn't happen you'd swiftly get fined five-thousand pounds.

After that the British Museum itself decided whether your find was what they called 'treasure trove'. Then they valued it and paid you the market value after which the amount was usually split between the farmer and the finders according to the agreement they had in place.

"And luckily, Jerry," Pete had said with a smile to his wife, "I've got that very agreement which you signed with me—right here."

And he'd taken out the piece of paper which—if this 'tray' was what he thought it was—would save the house, the farm, his livelihood and his family from going bust before the year was out.

He thought again. *How unlikely.*

Because Pete Butterworth was very broke indeed, and it seemed like only the miracle of hidden treasure would save him from financial meltdown. Lady Repton, who owned this land that Pete's family had farmed for three generations, had already made it clear that come April the rents were going up—again.

Professor Peregrine Cartwright laid down his magnifying glass, closed his notebook and surveyed the room dramatically.

Uh-oh, here comes the news, thought Pete. *What will it be?*

His heart was beating like a steam hammer.

"Firstly," said the elderly archaeologist, "I'd like to say that you acted correctly in calling me here this evening, Mr Butterworth. All historical finds must be correctly notified to the authorities as soon as possible. Requesting the assistance of an expert such as myself—albeit retired, I must add—to verify such finds always... how may I put it... oils the wheels of the relevant processes—"

"Eh?" said Baz.

"He means we've got to do this 'by the book' and he's going to help," said Jerry, as if he was a translator.

"Right," said Baz, though he still looked confused.

"If I may continue?"

"Please do, Professor," said Pete.

He realised that Cartwright was used to being in charge and decided he should just let him carry on. Becky moved round, pulled the chair out and sat next to him. Her hand reached for his under the table and she gave it a squeeze.

"Thank you so much," Cartwright continued smoothly. "Now, first of all we must establish the security of the site. Mr Butterworth, perhaps tomorrow you could get some fencing organised and hire in some additional help in advance of further excavation?"

Pete nodded, not sure where this was going.

"In the meantime, I shall contact the British Museum myself, first thing in the morning," said Cartwright. "Now, if the artefact is to stay here, you will need twenty-four-hour security. I can recommend a trusted service based in Oxford. They've done this type of thing before and you'll only need it for the weeks it takes the British Museum to kick into high gear."

Pete looked at his wife.

Round-the-clock security? How in the world could he pay for that? He had heard it could take a year to get the money from something like this.

There had to be another way.

"Professor, is there something else we might do? The bank perhaps. Could they—"

Cartwright produced a small laugh as if the idea was absurd.

"Banks steer clear of such things. Liability issues all over the place. But…"

Cartwright paused, and looked as though an idea had just occurred to him. He stroked his beard and nodded.

"There is one thing you might do. I could—perhaps—take it with me to my own house in Cherringham? I have a substantial safe designed specifically for the storage of such valuable objects. I suppose… I could adopt stewardship in this case."

"That would be excellent," Pete replied.

"Then we're agreed?"

"I think that's for the best," Pete looked to Becky for agreement. Luckily, she nodded.

"Hang on," said Jerry. "You mean you're going to *take* the tray? But it's ours!"

"My dear boy," said Professor Cartwright, "I couldn't possibly let *you* have charge of it."

"Why not? It's our tray. We found it."

"I do not dispute that fact. There is no argument about ownership here. Though I should perhaps disabuse you of the notion that this is a tray."

"Eh?" said Baz again.

"Professor Cartwright," Pete interjected, asking what he'd been dying to know since Jerry and Baz had brought it to him. "I just wonder if you could tell us what in fact it is?"

"Of course, of course!" Cartwright replied enthusiastically. "It's a rather fine example of fourth-century Roman silverware. A platter—or plate. Decorated with various marine deities, and with a fine Bacchus and some breathtakingly detailed Maenads."

"Silver?" said Jerry, sounding disappointed. "So, not gold then?"

"Of course not," Cartwright replied, as though the very suggestion was absurd.

"So not worth very much then?" said Baz, now looking rather downhearted.

"On the contrary, I would surmise it is worth rather a lot of money."

Pete's heart skipped a beat.

"Come on prof," said Jerry. "Let the monkey see the nuts! How much are we talking about?"

Professor Cartwright sighed as if the very notion of placing a value on a Roman artefact was the height of bad taste.

"Well... The Mildenhall Platter—a similar find from the forties—is far inferior in workmanship and quality. And the complete hoard was valued then at approximately fifty thousand pounds, if my recollection is correct."

Pete swallowed and felt his wife's hand squeeze his own tightly. Fifty thousand pounds! Even split down the middle, ten or twenty grand would be enough to get the family out of trouble. Across the table Jerry and Baz gave each other a high five.

"Result!" said Jerry. Then to Baz: "What I tell ya?"

"Wahey!" echoed Baz rubbing his hands together in glee.

Professor Cartwright coughed impatiently.

"However, with inflation to consider of course, you might confidently expect the plate to be valued by the authorities today at somewhere between one and one-and-a-half million."

Pete felt the blood drain from his face.

"Give or take a few hundred thousand," the professor added, as if playing with them.

At this the room went silent again and Pete could swear they had all stopped breathing. Professor Cartwright stood and looked down at them all.

"So we all agree that it is probably the wisest course of action that I take the plate—the Cherringham Plate as it will no doubt be known—and store it overnight in my safe?"

Pete was unable to speak. He looked at his wife and saw there were tears streaming down her face.

"Yes," he said, holding back the tears himself. "I'm sure you're right."

"Now if we can wrap it in some material, and help get it into my car… and then I'll be off."

4.

PARTY AT THE PLOUGHMAN'S

JACK BRENNAN PULLED his Austin Healey Sprite into a space off to the side of the Ploughman's car park, and killed the engine.

Just about the last free space. Must be some kind of celebration going on, he guessed. Maybe he should just head back to The Grey Goose, fix a martini and–

But no. One of his resolutions for the New Year—one which he had been good at keeping so far—was to start living more like a local and less like the visiting Yank.

He was singing in the Rotary Choir, which was a start… but what would a real Cherringham local do from time to time?

That's right: he'd stop in at the pub, have a chat with whoever might be there. Taking a deep breath, he got out of his sports car and walked up to the double doors of the classic pub.

IT DEFINITELY SEEMED like a party inside.

Jack nodded and smiled, seeing a few people that he had bumped into before, and also a lot of new faces. He navigated the crowds to a vacant spot at the bar where three people kept the beers flowing, the foamy heads of pints dotting the bar's countertop.

"Pint of bitter," Jack said with what he hoped seemed like practised ease.

The barmaid, Ellie, maybe the same age as his daughter, gave him a smile as she grabbed a glass and brought it to the old-fashioned pump. While she filled the glass, Jack turned and tried to figure out what was going on here.

Two men stood off to the right near the dart-board, seemingly the centre of attention.

One thin, wiry, the other all round and doughy. They were surrounded by people who, glasses held close, acted as though the two men were visiting royalty, when what they really looked like were down-on-their-luck farmhands.

"Here you go, Jack," Ellie said.

"Thanks," he said scooping up the pint, and vacating the bar, moving slightly closer to hear what the two men were talking about.

"SO, TOMORROW'S WHEN we find what's what. Ain't that right, Baz?"

The thin man nodded towards his friend who responded with a slur in his voice, indicating that he must have been putting away the pints rather quickly.

"Er... and we'll tell yers all how it went. Drinks on the house!"

One man in the crowd with a full grey beard that masked his face, turned to the group and shouted: "Hear that boys—drinks on the house!"

But Jack saw the thin guy quickly lose his smile and shoot Baz a look that said... *shut the hell up.*

Baz hurried to clarify.

"When we get our money. You bet. Just n-not now."

The old man with a beard seemed to deflate.

He had been that close to a free pint or two.

"The *perfessor*," the man continued, "says it could be worth a million. Maybe more."

The crowd produced a communal 'oooh'. That was a lot of money in Cherringham. A lot of money anywhere.

Jack turned to a young guy, dressed in overalls, skull cap on his head, listening.

"Excuse me—just curious… what's up with these guys? Win the lottery or something?"

The guy turned to Jack. "Nah, they found treasure! Roman. Worth tons."

"Really? And they have it here?"

The man shook his head. "Some professor guy has it. Safe keeping until the museum people come tomorrow."

"Big news for Cherringham," Jack said.

But the guy had gone back to listening to the two treasure hunters, now describing in detail exactly how it was found, milking their moment. Jack had a thought as he drained his pint. Could be there was an interesting local story here—and he knew just who to tell.

But first, maybe he'd get a bit more information.

HE WAITED UNTIL the crowd of people had thinned: the epic tale of the great discovery had come to an end and, with no free rounds on offer, people decided it was time to sail home.

The man called Baz was slumped on a chair in the corner while the other treasure hunter stood by the pool table, talking to a woman who was as round as he was thin.

Good time to find out more.

He walked over and stood by the two of them for a moment.

Finally the man looked up. Though tall, Jack had a good inch on him.

Jack gave him a smile.

"Congratulations," Jacks said, tilting his glass towards the man.

The man grinned back and clinked his near-empty glass.

"Jack Brennan. And quite the discovery, Mr—"

"Jerry Pratt," the man said. "Yeah, helluva find."

"Had a question."

The man's eyes narrowed. Up close, Jack realised that he had seen him at the Ploughman's before—not that he was someone to take note of.

Now though, with great wealth heading Jerry Pratt's way, it was a different story.

"Heard you have a professor looking after your find?"

Jerry told him about the safe, and how tomorrow they'd all be there when the safe was opened and the expert from the British Museum evaluated their prize.

"All? Beside you two, who would that be?"

"Pete, his farm. And Lady Repton, she owns the property."

"All get a cut?"

Jerry acted like he didn't like that thought, since his gaunt face screwed up again, lips pursed. Even with a million to be divided, who wants to share?

Humans are indeed funny when it comes to money, Jack thought.

Though maybe that wasn't exactly the right word.

Jack found out the professor's name—Peregrine Cartwright— but by that point Jerry looked suspicious. "Why all the questions?" he asked.

Jack smiled, hoping to defuse that suspicion. "Got a friend. She puts out the *Cherringham Roundel*, the online newsletter for the village."

Jack might as well been speaking Esperanto.

"Anyway, bet she'd like to cover that story, be there when the expert examines the plate, get your picture."

Jerry nodded. "Yeah, sure. Why not?"

"Good. Big news for Cherringham, right?"

The man leaned into Jack, not as bad as Baz, but still a bit wobbly. "Big damn news for me, that's all I know."

Then he laughed, turning back to the woman, all wide-eyed, standing in apparent adoration of a man who—though he looked like he was shy of two nickels to bang together—in truth might now be a millionaire.

Jack put his glass down on a nearby table and, with another nod to Jerry, headed out to the car, thinking.

Interesting night to drop in at the local. You never know…

"IT'S SOMETIME TOMORROW morning, Sarah," Jack said. "Think you can get an invite?"

Sarah sounded excited at Jack's idea. As she had told him, sending out the weekly online newsletter for Cherringham Council—filled with local updates and events—wasn't much of a gig, but she enjoyed putting it together.

And, he guessed, every penny counted. The discovery of the Roman artefact came as close to real 'news' as anything.

"I heard that Professor Cartwright had retired. Never met the man, seen him about the village. But I could try calling him."

"And the woman who actually owns the ground?"

Jack thought that this whole legal process of discovered treasure was incredibly convoluted and fussy.

Never fly in the States, he knew. Finders definitely keepers there.

"Lady Repton. Never met her either. The Reptons own a lot of the land round here—but word is they're struggling. This could save her."

"I'm guessing a lot of people are thinking just that."

"Jack—shall I try to get you an invite as well?

"No. I can read about in the *Cherringham Roundel*."

Sarah laughed. "Along with the results of the St James Bring-and-Buy Sale."

"Oh, that too." He looked around at the night sky, dotted with stars. It was getting late.

"I'll let you know how it goes," Sarah said.

"Great."

"And Jack—thanks for the heads-up."

"Sure. Speak soon."

The call ended, Jack paused another few moments, taking in the unusually clear sky.

He was struck with an amazing thought. That perhaps right here, on this ancient road down to the river, Roman legions marched by, camped out, battled local tribes.

I'm not in Kansas anymore, or the good old USA, he thought.

Coming to England and being surrounded by so much history made it seem more alive, somehow—just like that plate—buried a few feet underground, a marker left by an empire that once conquered this island.

Maybe tonight, he'd sit for a while and read some Gibbon. Not the easiest bit of reading, but he knew if you wanted to understand how empires rose and fell, Gibbon's history was the one to go to, even after all these years. And with that Jack walked to the Sprite, glad tonight to be a 'local'... and maybe even thinking it could be permanent.

5.

A SURPRISE AT THE PROFESSOR'S

SARAH SAT STRAIGHT-BACKED in Professor Peregrine Cartwright's sitting room.

Lady Repton occupied a leather chair, a walking stick held tightly in her right hand, with Cartwright by her side. They chatted quietly, while the men stood around the perimeter of the ornate room with its brilliant bronze walls and thick purple drapes, now pulled open, letting sun fill the room.

As for the men—*a motley crew indeed*, Sarah thought.

The two treasure finders looked as though they'd had a rough night, faces puffy, eyes sunken as if the morning sunlight streaming in might damage their brains.

The farmer—Pete Butterworth—looked nervous; fidgeting as he shifted on his feet, looked at his watch, checked his phone, then began the routine all over again.

Cartwright had seemed delighted when she called, excited that Sarah wanted to cover the evaluation for the *Cherringham Roundel*.

"It's only an online newsletter," she explained. "The Village council asked me to—"

"Of *course*. It's simply wonderful to have an event like this covered. Why, it's history coming to life!"

"And fortunes to be made," she said.

THICK AS THIEVES

"Er, yes that too. I will need to check with Lady Repton, of course, but I can't imagine she'd have any objections at all. The more attention we bring to this great find, the better!"

Enthusiastic didn't exactly capture the professor's response.

Except now the treasure evaluator from the British Museum was late. Apparently road trouble on the M40. He had sent Cartwright a text to say that he was close, but the delay had put everyone in the room on edge.

Sarah had the thought: *everyone here not only wants the money from this find—they* need *it.*

Just then the bell to Cartwright's cottage sounded and everyone snapped to; the discoverers doing their best to stand up straight, Pete Butterworth spinning around to face the front door.

Cartwright patted Lady Repton's hand, and with a big grin, he dashed to the front door.

Sarah thought: *this is exciting.*

And as if visiting royalty, the evaluator entered the room.

"EVERYONE, MAY I present Doctor Reginald Buchanan, with the Department of Portable Antiquities and Treasure at the British Museum."

Buchanan had a rotund physique that looked like a throwback to another century. *A 'bay-window' is what they used to call it,* Sarah thought. Wearing a vest which struggled to remain buttoned and sporting a carefully manicured moustache, he had the look of a man who had just stepped out of Mr Wells' time machine.

Something about their manner suggested to Sarah that Buchanan and Cartwright had met before. Made sense—the Oxford history professor and the antiquity expert…

"Cup of tea?"

Buchanan raised a hand.

The evaluator didn't seem too taken with Cartwright nor had he offered an apology to the assembled group for his delay.

"No," he said, turning the two-letter word into an elongated call one might use to attract an owl.

Buchanan looked around at the group, making no effort to hide his disdain at the audience for the artefact's unveiling. Then he looked at Sarah, and she popped to her feet.

"Sarah Edwards" she said, holding out her hand. "I'm writing about this for our local newsletter, the—"

But with a nod, Buchanan turned away.

"Well, let's get on with it. If you have something real, something of *value*, I will need considerable time to examine it very carefully."

He repeated these words.

"Very carefully… to note its condition, to be exactly sure what you have here."

"It's the real bloody thing," Jerry Pratt spurted. "You can be sure of that."

The room fell silent. The opinion of one of the men who had wielded the metal detector, trolling mud for treasure, didn't carry any weight here.

Cartwright pulled another chair close to the wall, near Lady Repton.

He clapped his hands together.

"Very well. Then we shall proceed. I've prepared my dining room table so you'll have room to examine the item, evaluate it."

Cartwright walked over to a painting on the right side of the room, where the ceiling-high bookshelves ended. The painting looked vaguely Klimt-like: two figures covered in patches of gold and silver facing each other, embracing.

A little garish, Sarah thought. *Hardly classic.*

Cartwright pulled at a corner of the painting and it swung open like a door, revealing a safe as big as the painting, and a complex combination lock at dead centre.

Then, with a schoolboy grin, he turned back to everyone. "I do hope I remember the combination!"

A quick look left and right showed that no one found any humour in the professor's not-so-*bon mots*.

Cartwright turned to the combination lock and began fiddling with the dial, muttering to himself as he did.

"Left, right, left again, and—"

He grabbed the latch but the door didn't move at all.

"Sorry," he said, turning back to his audience. "The lock's very fussy. It has to be exactly on the right spot. Okay. Another go."

Sarah looked over at Buchanan who seemed poised to crush the chair that held him. Like a miscast group of actors, the other potential recipients of the money—save for Lady Repton—stood near the back, as if ready to pounce once the safe popped open.

Lady Repton's eyes—Sarah noted—were locked squarely on Cartwright's fumbling.

If I wrote this up just as it's happening now, it would make for an exciting piece for the newsletter. Sadly, not to be.

The *Roundel*'s tone—as requested by the Council—was to be clearly informative, matter of fact, with a smidge of exuberance for good deeds done and the triumphant nights of amateur theatricals and music recitals.

"Left, and—"

Cartwright had finished another attempt to open the safe. This time, moving more slowly, he reached up and pulled down hard on the handle to the safe, gave it a yank.

It went fully down with a resounding *click*.

Even the jaded Buchanan leaned forward slightly, waiting for the big reveal.

Cartwright swung open the door slowly, and then reached in.

"Wha—"

For a moment Sarah suspected Cartwright was providing a moment of ill-timed play as he 'searched' for the plate.

But then, his head peered inside, even vanishing into the open maw of the safe while his hands noisily flapped around.

In the garishly decorated sitting room you could hear the proverbial pin drop.

Only the next sound wasn't a pin.

Cartwright spun around as if he had seen the dead come to life, lower lip trembling, eyes darting as he gave the news that no one wanted to hear.

"It's *gone*! The treasure is gone!"

6.

MAYHEM IN THE MORNING

FOR A MOMENT Sarah thought she'd be knocked over in the ensuing tumult.

Jerry and Baz, hungover as they were, came to life as if jolted with a massive bolt of electricity. They ran to the safe, literally pushing the professor to the side as they fought to stick their two heads into the opening.

Lady Repton remained sitting—but now Sarah saw that she had another use for her cane, as she raised it shakily and started pointing at Cartwright, her gravelly, froggy voice demanding: "Where the hell is it, Cartwright? What have you done with my treasure?"

The farmer, Butterworth—who had seemed the steadiest of the group—didn't move at all. But he kept looking around the room as if someone had siphoned off all the oxygen and in minutes he'd fall down onto the thick curlicues of what must be an expensive Persian rug, suffocating.

Cartwright had staggered away, his now-shaky hands using the rich wood of the bookshelves to steady himself, muttering quietly at first but then—in case anyone didn't hear—raising his voice.

"I've been robbed. Good God, someone has… *robbed* me!"

Not exactly the item I had planned on writing, Sarah thought.

And lastly there was Buchanan.

Had he ever experienced a scene like this? Or was this an everyday occurrence in the life of the esteemed representative of the British Museum?

Either way, without revealing his thoughts on what was unfolding, he stood up.

"This," he announced, his voice rich, commanding, "is not a matter to be trifled with. Professor, you others. A treasure has been found, and now—this... *charade*?"

He said the last word with disgust.

Cartwright ran from the wall to Buchanan who was already navigating his blimp-sized physique to the door.

"This is impossible! I have alarms. And that safe, it's top-of-the-line, one of the best."

Buchanan didn't let the entreaties slow his progress to the door out of the house.

But Pete Butterworth put a hand on the evaluator's shoulder. "What will happen? What's going to happen now?"

Buchanan turned to him. "Why, I shall report to the Museum and the relevant authorities and you lot must report this absolutely immediately to the local constabulary. The item must be found, and whoever did this—"

A pregnant pause delivered with all the force Buchanan could muster.

"Well, let's say they have made a serious error. You do not trifle with a treasure of the Queen!"

And with that he shrugged off Butterworth's hand.

Jerry and Baz returned from their caving expedition in the empty safe. They went to Cartwright, one on each side.

"You *said* it would be safe, you old fool!" Jerry yelled, his mouth mere inches from the man's right ear.

"This is on you, *Perfesser*," said Baz. "You'll answer for this, you will!"

And to bring the point fully home, Baz jabbed his finger at the tip of Cartwright's nose.

"Stop that you buffoon!" Cartwright yelled.

Even Lady Repton tried to get in on the accosting Cartwright game, but her cane couldn't reach the man. Still, she waved it in the air, from Cartwright to Buchanan.

"This is a robbery. The Museum must help us—"

At that Buchanan, Burberry already on, turned to her.

"I'm afraid, M'Lady, that the Museum only gets involved when there are artefacts to be examined, evaluated. In this case, it appears there is nothing but fraud, theft. That's all I can evaluate here! Either way, not in my bailiwick. If your plate surfaces, you know how to reach me."

And with his exit line expertly delivered, the man from London left.

Which to Sarah—seeing the entire crowd yelling at each other, accusing one, then the other—seemed like exactly the right thing to do.

She sprang from her chair and, without anyone taking any notice at all, Sarah dashed to the door and out into the chilly spring air outside, now amazingly refreshing.

7.

TEA FOR TWO

SARAH AND JACK sat at a table at the back of Huffington's, which was already beginning to fill with a lunch crowd.

Jack was laughing, wiping his tears from his eyes.

When he stopped: "Oh, I wish I'd been there."

"Best of all was the expert from the museum. Straight out of Oscar Wilde."

Jack shook his head. "More than a million. Gone, just like that."

"If it was the real thing, of course."

"Well," said Jack. "There is that."

Sarah nodded. As the place filled, it was hard to have a private conversation. People at the tearooms tended to chat to their friend, then—eyes darting left and right—they checked out the other conversations orbiting their table.

She lowered her voice.

"Anyway, the police have now had a week to investigate and guess what their verdict is?"

"You tell me," said Jack.

"According to today's paper, they are 'following a number of promising lines of enquiry and welcome any information which will be treated in the strictest confidence'."

"Ah."

"Ah, indeed!" said Sarah, laughing. "They haven't got a clue—right?"

"You know me—I'm never one to knock the cops but…"

"But?"

"But that sounds to me like they've hit a dead end."

"I agree," said Sarah. "They're hinting it's the work of a gang that's been breaking into country houses in the area, stealing art works."

"Hmm. Seems unlikely. Gangs like that tend to plan ahead, not jump in."

"So what do *you* think happened?"

Jack looked around him as though for inspiration. "Don't rightly know. Not having met the 'players' so to speak. From what you described, seems like they all had a motive for stealing the plate."

"But it was in the safe, locked away, and—"

Jack held up a hand. "According to Cartwright. We only have his word."

"He opens his safe, and it's empty. Wouldn't that make him the main suspect?"

"Funny thing about safes, they can be opened."

Jack took a sip of his Earl Grey. One sweetener, no milk.

Sarah knew his tastes nearly as well as her own.

"So it could have been a robbery?"

"Could have. If someone knew it was there. Or—even if they didn't." Another smile. "A nice surprise."

Sarah shook her head. "I don't know. I can't picture those two lads with their detectors figuring out how to do that. And Lady Repton? I think she has enough of a challenge opening the front door to her manor house. I suppose Butterworth could—"

"Butterworth?"

"The farmer. Rents the place from Lady Repton. He seems

pretty competent."

Jack cleared his throat. He too seemed aware that the place was filling with people, people likely picking up an intriguing word here or there.

"Here's the thing: you'd be surprised what people can do. The two guys who found it? Maybe they know someone more, um, capable. And Lady Repton? If there is big money on offer, even the crotchety dowager could find an accomplice. Then there's the professor. His home, his safe—"

"He definitely seemed surprised."

Jack grinned. "From your description of him, I think acting could be one of his many talents." He took the last bite of his small chocolate cake, a bit of dark icing sticking to his lips, which he quickly wiped away. "These cakes, they're addictive. If I ever start coming here every day, stage an intervention."

"Absolutely."

Then she saw Jack looking at her. "Let me guess, you're feeling like you want to, um, do some investigating?"

At that she broke into a smile. What they had done in the past, looking into unsolved crimes, had been so exciting and—better yet—it had worked. People had been caught, crimes solved.

And this? Such a major heist.

"Things in the office *are* a little slow," she said. "So I do have some time. And it would make a great follow-up to my story on the robbery."

"Tell you what," he paused, taking another look around the room. "I've been meaning to have—I dunno—a little soiree on the Goose. Invite some people I've met here. Drinks and—what do you call them here… nibbles?"

"Sounds nice."

"Show people I appreciate their not treating me as if I just walked off an American spaceship. Feeling accepted, you know?"

"You're not the oddity you were when you arrived."

Another smile from Jack. "Thank you for that. Been trying to fit in. So, a little party. Gives me a good excuse to clean the boat. Single guy… it's gotten a bit messy."

"Need me to give you a hand?"

"I'm good with the cleaning, thanks. But planning the party, what to have, who to invite? The precise nature of the nibbles? With that, I could use some help."

"Of course," she said, laughing.

"Well in that case, I'd be glad to dig into this a bit with you. Still early for fishing anyway."

Sarah smiled. "Great. So where do we start?"

"I'd love to hear what the police have to say."

"A visit to Alan?" said Sarah.

On a previous case, Alan, who Sarah had known for years, hadn't seemed too happy with Jack and Sarah's involvement in— what he called—strictly police matters. Still, she knew Alan liked her and, better yet, Jack's former superiors had in the past put in a useful call to Alan's supervisors.

"One for you I think," said Jack.

"And you?" said Sarah, finishing her tea.

"I want to look into how this treasure law works. Figuring that out might explain who'd want that plate so badly… and exactly what they would do with it."

"I think the renowned Professor Cartwright is the man you need."

And with people waiting for a free table, Sarah stood up, and she left Huffington's with Jack talking about stolen treasure, and wondering where this trail might lead them.

SARAH WATCHED JACK drive off in his little sports car, his hand raised in a cheerful wave. Who would she invite to his drinks party? This was going to be fun...

But first—they had a robbery to solve.

She walked up the High Street, passing the shops on the Square—the little art gallery, the antiques shop, the organic grocers—until she reached the squat old building that was the police station.

Above the door, carved deep in the warm Cotswold stone, were the words 'Police Station and Petty Sessions'—left over from the days when arrest, justice and punishment were all effectively delivered in the one building.

She pushed open the door and entered the secure lobby.

Years ago, when she was a kid in the village, there was just a worn old oak countertop in here to separate the forces of law and order from the unruly villagers.

Or, in her day, drunk teenagers.

Now, automatic door-locks, a sheet of armoured glass and a microphone system were required.

Have we really changed that much? wondered Sarah.

In truth they were lucky to still have a police station at all. Most of the surrounding villages had lost theirs and were now dependent on sporadic visits from patrol cars whose drivers came from the nearest city.

"Sarah!" the uniformed policeman behind the glass welcomed her in.

"Hi Alan," said Sarah.

At least I know my local cop, she thought. *Maybe too well.*

Sarah had gone to school with Alan, and from the age of thirteen onwards he had made it clear he fancied her. She knew that he still did, but no matter how many times she'd made it clear he just wasn't her type, it seemed he still clung to the hope that one day she'd see the light.

These days though, his forlorn love was also mixed with irritation at her ventures into crime-busting.

"Now then," he said through the armoured glass. "You're not here to report a stolen bike."

"Nope."

"Or complain about a parking ticket."

Sarah smiled innocently. "Nope."

"And there aren't any murders to report." He shook his head. "Or to investigate."

"Nope."

"So let me guess... You want to know about the break-in at Professor Cartwright's, don't you?"

"Yes!" said Sarah. "That's amazing Alan. Have you ever thought of joining—"

"—the police force?" he asked, wryly. "These days I wonder why you didn't!"

Alan pressed the button to release the door and nodded to her to come through.

"Come on, I could do with a cuppa anyway."

"Oh me too—I'm parched," said Sarah, although in truth the last thing she wanted was another cup of tea.

She followed him through, the door clicking shut behind her. Tucked away behind tall filing cabinets was a small kitchen area, with an old table and a couple of chairs.

"Sit yourself down," said Alan, putting the kettle on.

He made the tea in mugs, set them down on the table and sat opposite her.

"So, who's asked you to get involved this time?" he said wearily.

"Actually—nobody," said Sarah. "You know I was there when the robbery was discovered?"

"I seem to remember reading your statement," said Alan. "It was pretty funny to be honest."

"I tell it how I see it."

"You haven't changed."

Sarah could sense the deeper meaning but moved on.

"Anyway—I want to write something up for the village online news and the police statement in the paper just said, well, nothing. So I thought you might tell me a bit more. You know—old pals and all that?"

"Hmm, old pals…"

Alan stared levelly at her and Sarah worked hard to keep her smile open and cheerful.

He shrugged.

"All right. Off the record, eh? Truth is—we haven't really found anything."

"I thought it was being pinned on the gang that's been doing country houses these last few months?"

"CID put that out," he said. "Makes the stats look better—not that I quite understand how."

"So there's no real evidence?"

"Not that I've heard."

"Sounds like you're not working on it?" said Sarah, suddenly seeing an angle.

"No. It's gone over to Oxford. Out of our hands."

"That doesn't seem fair."

Alan shrugged. Sarah knew she had to be careful what she said here.

"You know, Alan, if we found out anything…"

"We? You mean you and that American?"

"Yeah—me and Jack," she said slowly. "We'd pass it straight to you. We wouldn't go to CID."

She watched Alan think this over. He knew exactly what she was suggesting—and she could tell that he needed the kudos.

"All I want is what's in the crime report," she said. "Wouldn't go any further. And if there's a collar—you get it. Cherringham gets it—not Oxford."

Alan paused to reflect.

Then she watched, curious, as he got up, opened one of the filing cabinets and flicked through the contents. Finding what he wanted, he came back and laid a file on the table in front of Sarah.

"I've just got to go and fill out a form at the front desk," he said. "I'll only be five minutes. When you've had your tea, come on through."

He left the kitchen area and went back to the counter. Sarah reached for the file and spun it round so she could read it.

It was the crime report on the theft at Professor Peregrine Cartwright's.

8.

A VISIT WITH THE PROFESSOR

JACK SHUFFLED UNCOMFORTABLY in his seat and waited for Professor Cartwright to hand him his tea.

Regency chairs might have been comfortable back in the eighteenth century if you were rail thin, but Jack's body, shaped by thirty years of NY-deli breakfasts, was a tough squeeze into the little gold-and-yellow frame and he hoped that the chair's legs were stronger than they looked.

He took the tiny bone-china cup and for once rejected the offer of sugar.

Professor Cartwright sat back on the sofa and faced him, his expression—at least to Jack's experienced eye—one of unconcealed disdain.

"Mr Brennan, let me be clear. We are having this discussion for one reason and one reason only."

"That is?"

"The theft of the Roman plate has been deeply embarrassing for me, in both a professional and personal capacity. And while the police regard the matter as just 'one more in a series' of robberies across the county—and in my opinion are treating this whole affair in a dilatory fashion—I shall not be at ease until the culprits are found and the artefact recovered."

"So—any offer of help is welcome, huh?"

"Precisely. Even yours."

Jack decided to ignore the barb and carry on in his chosen 'jovial Yank' mode.

"And people are blaming you for the robbery?" he offered.

"There have been comments—among the faculty, I gather."

"That seems pretty unfair."

"Academics can be ruthless, Mr Brennan. As merciless as any hardened criminal when they sense weakness."

"And you are in a weak position?"

"Apparently. It seems I... er... omitted one or two formalities in the customary process of registering treasure trove. But I acted as I did in good faith, in order to accelerate the procedure and more quickly bring an extraordinary artefact to the attention of the relevant authorities."

This guy swallowed more than a dictionary, thought Jack, working hard to translate.

"Of course," Jack said, with a small smile. "Just to be straight—you should have photographed the plate and then contacted the local authorities."

"Those are the recommendations for the layman, Mr Brennan."

"For Joe Public you mean?"

"Exactly. But I am hardly 'Joe Public'. I was for twenty years Emeritus Professor of Classical Archaeology at the University of Oxford. I have a long-standing professional relationship with the British Museum who would have been called in immediately anyway. And I am one of the leading experts—if not *the* leading expert in this country in Romano-British history."

"Impressive."

"I think you would agree that in my case those minor regulations need hardly apply."

"Romano-British?"

"Ah, I forget. You're a colonial. I refer to the period between 43 and 409 when Britain was a province of the Roman Empire, until the latter's tragic decline. I presume you are familiar with the Roman Empire, Mr Brennan?"

"A little," said Jack. "And you know what? I'm kinda with Gibbon on that one: 'The history of empires is the history of human misery'."

Professor Peregrine Cartwright blinked.

"Ah. Yes," he said. "*Decline and Fall.* Well, well."

Jack quietly notched up a score for the Colonials.

"Perhaps you could show me how you think the burglars made their entry?" he said, putting down his tea cup on a side table and giving Professor Cartwright his biggest smile.

JACK CROUCHED DOWN by the open kitchen door and carefully inspected the broken pane of glass in the panel to the side of the frame.

The local glass company had put a board in, but it was clear that the glass had been smashed so the intruder could reach in and turn the door handle.

"The break-in happened some time during the night? And you were here?"

"That would be the logical assumption, don't you think? Since the plate was in the safe when I retired and it was gone when I looked in the morning."

If this guy was my teacher I'd have decked him before the end of the first term, thought Jack.

"And you didn't hear anything during the night?"

"No. I went to bed early. And I use earplugs on a Saturday night. Even Cherringham is not immune from teenage revellers, Mr Brennan."

"And in the morning you didn't notice the glass was smashed?"

"I confess not. It was a mild day. I was only briefly in the kitchen before my guests arrived."

"No glass on the floor?"

"Not that I noticed. Of course, once I was aware that the plate was gone, I looked around, spotted the glass and realised I'd been burgled."

"So other stuff was taken?"

"Oh yes. Some miniatures. Silverware from one of the drawers. And coins—but fortunately nothing too rare."

"You were insured, I take it?"

"Of course. But not for the plate. Its value was unknown— or at least, not certified. And it was in my secure safe!"

Jack paused to think.

"Shall we have a look at the other door?"

Cartwright turned and headed back through the kitchen into the house.

"This way."

Jack followed him down the hallway to the heavy oak front door. The professor opened it and pointed to the door catch.

"You see the scratches?" he said. "The police believe the gang tried to gain entry here first by slipping the lock—but failed. Thus forcing them to enter via the back door."

42

Jack could see the brass catch was scored, and the edge of the door itself had scrapes on the paint.

He looked down the front garden towards the village square just twenty or so yards away. A path led straight to a picket gate and a tall hedge. Trimmed lawns and a pair of apple trees shaded the path. Shrubs around the porch would have given good cover for anyone trying to break in.

No surprise that even on a busy night the burglars had been able to work unnoticed.

"Let's go look at the safe," said Jack, not waiting for Professor Cartwright and heading towards the sitting room.

SARAH HAD TOLD Jack about the big safe behind the painting, but he wasn't prepared for its size.

While the professor muttered to himself and fiddled with the combination dial, Jack took in the room. Would burglars know that the safe was behind this painting?

On balance—if they knew what they were looking for—he thought, yes. There were no other large paintings and the frame seemed discoloured where, over time, Cartwright's hand had taken off the varnish. Right now the professor seemed to be having difficulty getting the thing to open. He tugged at the brass handle but nothing happened.

"Damn this—"

"Having trouble, Professor?"

Jack heard the academic tut-tut again as he went to the desk. He pulled out a thin pen-tray built into the frame, withdrew a slip of paper. A quick look, a nod, and then he slipped the paper and tray back into the desk and went back to the safe to try again.

Jack shook his head.

"I hope you don't mind me asking this, Professor—but do you actually have the combination written down?"

"Of course, dear boy. How else would I remember it?"

Jack went over to the desk and slid out the tray. Clearly written on a small tab of paper was a series of numbers and letters.

"Did you tell the police that the combination was in here?"

"I did not," said Professor Cartwright, indignantly. "I don't want the whole village to know the number, do I?"

Jack took a deep breath.

"No Professor, you don't. That would be just careless, wouldn't it?"

The irony was totally lost on the scholar.

Throughout his career as a cop in New York, often dealing with the brightest and the best talent that was drawn to that great City from around the world, it had never ceased to amaze Jack how stupid the cleverest of people could be.

But he had to admit, in Professor Cartwright, Emeritus Professor at the University of Oxford (retired), he'd found himself an absolute zinger.

9.

DRILL DOWN

SARAH OPENED THE last of Jack's galley cupboards and drew a blank.

The guy clearly liked to cook—there was no end of spices, herbs, and food groups from all around the world, some she'd never even heard of. But in terms of crockery, all she'd found so far were a couple of wine glasses, and she was going to need more than that.

She added another note to the planning list on her phone.

Turning Jack's boat into a party venue was going to involve some fairly extensive trips to the supermarket. Jack's voice came through the hatch from the deck above:

"Coffee's getting cold, Sarah—you nearly done?"

"On my way," she answered, and climbed the little ladder up into the spring sunshine.

Jack had cleaned the windows and swabbed the decks.

Swabbed... she thought. *Is that the right word?*

The old boat was looking a lot better than it had in the depths of winter. He'd set up a teak garden table and chairs on the deck with an umbrella and she could see that if the weather held out until the weekend then this area would make the perfect venue.

The river was flat calm and, in the distance, up on the far hill, just a few fluffs of cloud floated above Cherringham.

She sat at the table and Jack poured her coffee into what he called the 'visitor's mug'. Riley ambled up from the dog bed that lay to one side and offered his head on her lap for his customary ear scratching.

"So—you got the whole thing planned?" said Jack, sitting back in his chair. "I sure hope so! This party is beginning to scare me."

"I'll send you an email, Jack. Let's just say you're going to have your work cut out over the next few days." She laughed. "But don't worry, I'll help."

"Ah, well. About time I brought the Grey Goose up to a proper sociable standard."

A big white cruiser chugged slowly by, moving upriver, and the family behind the wheel gave a wave.

Sarah and Jack waved back.

"First warm weekend brings the vacation boats out," said Jack.

"You mind them invading your patch?"

"Heck, I like it," said Jack. "River's here to be used. Shared. Gives me something to look at too—free entertainment some days I can tell you."

Sarah sat back in her chair too, feeling the first real warmth of the year on her face.

Bliss.

"So Ms Detective," said Jack. "What's next in our search for the infamous Cherringham Plate?"

"I was hoping maybe you'd have a few ideas."

"No such luck," said Jack. "Like I said—all I learned at Professor Cartwright's house was that a fine education doesn't make you a clever guy. Anyone who really wanted to crack that safe could have done it without breaking into a sweat."

"Then the police might be right about the gang?"

"They might be. Though the failed attempt at the front door followed by the smashed window kinda nags at me. Not sure why though."

"You think the professor could have been involved?"

Jack shrugged.

"Sure, he *could* have been. But he's got a lot to lose and nothing to gain as far as I can see—I mean why would a guy with his reputation steal an artefact like that? He could dine out on identifying the great find for life. And how does he sell it?"

"That's true for whoever's stolen it. What about the others?"

"I don't buy it. And Lady Repton? That seems like a stretch."

"So it's a dead end?" said Sarah.

"For now," said Jack. "Which means?"

Sarah knew where this was going.

She'd already picked up a lot of techniques from the New York cop—and no small number of principles.

"It means we go back to basics," she answered. "Talk to everyone. Find out where all the possible suspects were on the night of the theft. Work out who's got a motive. See who needs the money."

"Exactly," said Jack. "Drill down."

"Who do you fancy on your dance card?"

"Farmer Butterworth, I think. Take a look at his field of silver."

"Okay," said Sarah. "How about you invite young Jerry out for a drink?"

Jack laughed.

"Maybe his pal Baz as well?"

"Which leaves Lady Repton for me."

"Shame. There was I thinking I'd have myself a one-to-one with nobility and maybe invite her over to my little drinks party too."

"Who knows. All options open. She might be the thief, Jack."

"From what I've read about the English upper classes Sarah, that's quite likely these days. But even if she's guilty, you know what? I'd still invite her. Felons can be quite interesting."

"You Americans, still suckers for the English aristocracy."

"Sure," said Jack. "Just so long as they can't tell us what to do."

"Talking of invites," said Sarah, taking out her phone. "Shall we see if we can put a list together for Saturday?"

Jack leaned back in his chair and put his hands behind his head, lazily.

"I guess so. But you know, sitting here with the river just waking up and the sun in the sky, I'm kinda wishing I didn't have to throw a party. Maybe I should put it off till next month?"

With two kids at home, Sarah had heard these kind of thoughts many times before and she knew just how to deal with them.

"Nonsense, Jack. Soon as people turn up you'll have the time of your life. Now let's get started, shall we?"

And just like a school-kid, Jack shrugged, sat forward, put his elbows on the table and rested his head in his hands.

"Yes, ma'am."

10.

DOWN ON THE FARM

JACK PULLED UP in the yard of Low Copse Farm and turned the engine off.

He looked around. Although he was a city boy, his grandparents had had a farm—and he knew enough from those childhood memories to recognise a well-run outfit.

This place looked tidy enough. Bales of straw still left over from the winter neatly stacked. Tractors lined up. No piles of scrap in forgotten corners, jumbles of metal or old sleepers.

The door to the farm opened and a tall man in his forties came out, crossed the yard to greet him.

"Mr Brennan? Pete Butterworth."

Jack shook his outstretched hand. He liked the guy already— some instinct at work there.

"It's Jack. Good of you to see me."

"Couldn't resist, to be honest. My wife and I have heard about some of your exploits—and we felt if anyone could find the plate— you could."

Jack rarely felt awkward—but he did now. The whole private detective thing conflicted with his natural desire to keep a low profile.

"Well, I wouldn't count on anything, Pete," he said quickly. "So far, it looks to me like the police are on the right track."

Behind Pete Butterworth, a woman appeared from the front of the house, wiping her hands on a tea towel. Pete turned to introduce her.

"Jack—my wife, Becky."

Jack shook her hand.

"Have you found out anything, Jack?"

"Not yet. In fact, I was just saying—I think you're going to be dependent on the police for that."

His words clearly had a depressing effect on both of them—had they been expecting him to be bringing good news? And was this tidy little farm perhaps not as serene as might first appear?

He decided to jump straight in.

"I hope you don't mind me asking—but does this find mean a lot to you?"

Becky Butterworth was quick to answer.

"Life or death—is that a lot?"

"I wouldn't go that far, love—" interrupted her husband.

"Well, isn't it? Life at least—our lives here at the farm."

Pete put his arm around his wife's shoulders.

"We don't own this farm, Jack. We're just tenants. Third generation, mind you, but that doesn't protect us. If we can't pay the rent each year, we lose the place."

"Then your share of the treasure trove would have helped you stay on?"

"More than that. You see in June we hit our three-year rent review and the owners of the land—"

"Lady Repton?" said Jack.

"The Repton family, yes," said Becky.

"They've already made it clear they're going to have to raise the rent to cover repairs they need to make to Repton House," continued Pete. "Raise it more than we could possibly afford."

Becky looked away, out to the fields, perhaps—Jack thought—imagining it all vanishing.

"Our share of the value of the plate would have kept us safe on this land not just for us—but for our kids too when they grow up and want to farm it."

I do like this guy, Jack thought. *Not that it rules him out.*

"That's tough," said Jack. "And for a day and a night you must have felt you were saved?"

"Too right," said Pete.

"I guess you must have celebrated there and then?" suggested Jack carefully.

But just when he was expecting both of them to start on a story of champagne bottles and going out for dinner, he saw straight away a nervous look between them. A look that he had seen so many times in interviews.

Something wrong here.

Could be a look that indicated a lie.

"Well, we, er…" started Becky.

"I had to get up early for milking next day, so we just had an early dinner. Extra beer. Just the one," said Pete, looking to Becky for confirmation.

"Went to bed early," she said, still nervously avoiding Jack's eye.

"Best to be cautious, huh?" said Jack.

"Exactly," said Pete.

He waited for them to say more, but he could see that they just clammed up.

"Tell you what," Jack said. "Why don't you show me where your two treasure hunters found this famous plate? The police are good, Pete, Becky. They may well get it back."

Nothing in their eyes showed that either of the couple had any hope in that.

"Love to see the spot. That way—when we get it back I can say I was part of the story."

"Sure," said Pete. "I'll bring the Land Rover round."

The farmer headed over to one of the barns where the vehicle was kept. Jack turned to Becky Butterworth.

"Guess Pete would do anything to get his hands on that plate, huh?"

Just the slightest nod from Becky, then she thanked him for visiting and made her goodbyes, turning back into the farmhouse.

He'd take a quick look at the spot where the plate had been found, he decided. Then, onto the next in line of the lucky quartet, now probably all feeling anything *but* lucky.

11.

A VISIT WITH THE FAMILY

JACK COULDN'T QUITE remember when he'd last held a baby in his arms, but he could remember how nervous the experience always made him.

And wow, this one was a wriggler.

Luckily it only took a moment for Baz and Abby—the little girl's parents—to clear a space in the tiny flat for Jack to sit and soon, with some relief, he was handing the little creature back to her mother.

"Sorry about that, mate," said Baz. "Chaos this place."

"First child—always hits like a hurricane," said Jack, thinking back to his own daughter who wasn't so little any more.

"Too bleeding right," said Abby. "No way I'm having another. Not unless we win the lottery. Or," she paused, her tone suddenly bitter, "find some hidden treasure, eh?"

This last remark was clearly aimed at Baz.

The baby suddenly quieted, and turned to look at Jack, eyes wide and—like all babies—irresistible.

"You should be proud," Jack said, meaning it.

And at the same time not sure these two were heading towards 'Parents of the Year' awards.

"Cup of tea?" Abby said.

"Or something stronger?" Baz added.

Jack gave the beleaguered couple a smile. "I'm good, thanks."

If ever two people looked like they needed a windfall, it was this couple.

"Baz, I wonder—I know how much that treasure might have meant to the both of you. Could I ask you some questions?"

In response, Baz's wife took a chair and sat down, eyes locked on Jack.

She—for one—was ready.

Baz looked around the room as if cornered.

He put his hand on the back of the wooden kitchen chair and slowly pulled it back from the table with a fraction of the speed of his wife.

Tad more reluctant, Jack saw.

Baz sat down, cleared his throat.

"Sure. Anything that can get it back for us. I mean, we know who you are, what you've done."

"That night at the Ploughman's. You told a lot of people about what you found and who had it."

"Stupid, bloody—" Abby muttered.

Baz seemed to wilt in the wooden chair.

"Well, yeah, me and Jerry were celebrating. Guess we got a little carried away."

Abby tilted her head in Baz's direction as if about shoot a laser from her eyes right into her husband's thick skull.

"You and your big mouth. Letting everyone know we were going to be rich. La-de-da! And even where the prize was."

"Yeah, that might have been a mistake," Jack said.

Baz pleaded his case. "But they're our mates! We've known those guys for ever. Who'd want to steal from us? Besides with it safe and sound in the professor's safe we thought——"

"Safe? Sound?" Abby interrupted, snorting.

"In that group of 'mates', Baz," Jack carried on, ignoring Abby. "Is there anyone at all you know that might have thought about stealing the plate?"

Baz shook his head quickly, showing that he had allotted no time to think of his answer.

"No. All mates. Most of them." He hesitated, thoughts catching up with tongue. "I mean, I dunno, I guess anybody could——"

"Too right," Abby agreed. "Anybody could have heard you two idiots, and planned the theft. Isn't that right, Jack?"

Jack now wondered if he might have been better off having these two still address him as 'Mr Brennan'.

Not sure I want to be chummy with them.

The baby burped, making Jack smile.

The moment was lost on the two parents.

"Okay," Jack said, "We know that a lot of people knew about the treasure and where it was being kept." He took a breath. "Can I ask you about the rest of that night?"

Because though Jack thought it unlikely, he couldn't rule out Baz wanting the treasure all to himself.

"You were—as we say—under the weather?" Jack continued.

"We was celebrating, that's all——"

"I get that. Who wouldn't?"

Jack looked at Abby hoping she didn't fire off another volley since that wouldn't help this process at all.

"What about the rest of the evening?"

Baz shifted in his seat.

"As you say, I was a bit wobbly. So Jerry said I could take his couch. Sleep it off. Didn't want to disturb the missus, and little Daisy here."

"More like you couldn't get your two damn feet to move in a straight line. That Jerry, he's an *enabler*, that's what he is."

"Best mate," Baz added for clarification.

The baby started squirming again, obviously in need of feeding or a change. Abby excused herself with the little girl and Jack spotted an opportunity to get in a few questions to Baz without Abby's commentary.

He pulled his chair closer to where Baz sat. A window of opportunity here, and he'd best jump on it.

"THAT NIGHT, YOU remember…?"

"Hitting Jezzer's couch. I was flat out, mate. Next morning, woke with a massive head. I mean, you saw me in the pub. Too much damn celebrating."

"Yeah, I could see that. Your friend though—he seemed better."

"Jezzer? Yeah, I mean I guess so."

"And do you know what he did? After he brought you to his place?"

Baz seemed surprised by the question.

"Whadya mean? He went to sleep, same as me. Didn't see him until the morning. That's what we did. Just crashed at his place until the morning, when the museum bloke was to come."

Jack nodded.

Then he felt he should point out the obvious to Baz.

That is, if Baz didn't already know it.

"But since you were flat out, on the couch, then there is no way you would know what Jerry did, right?"

"He said he went to sleep, same as me."

"But no way you would know for sure?"

Baz stopped as if some distant chamber in his brain, long unused, maybe even unknown, suddenly lit up with dusty light bulbs flickering to life.

Baz looked away. "I mean, no, but I guess… he could have—"

Jack finished the thought: "–done anything?"

The treasure hunter turned to him and his eyes looked sick, sunken and now more than a bit confused, and he nodded. Jack guessed that the interview was over, though he wasn't sure that he'd learned anything of any use.

But he also thought that speaking to Jerry next might be quite interesting.

Always fun to compare stories.

12.

A CONFLICTING OPINION

THE SUN HAD reached a point where it squarely hit the front window of Sarah's office, making her office desks and worktables—piled high with paper and layouts from a half dozen projects—look positively golden.

A good spring day in Cherringham is something amazing, Sarah thought.

As if the icy grip of winter, the leafless trees, the days of freezing rain had suddenly been banished, blown away by the glorious sun, making everything come back to life.

And business was good!

Maybe the economic doldrums were indeed over. Local shops wanted websites designed, and lots of posters were needed for spring sales, events—and she even had a major website build on the go for the grisly tourist attraction, Penton Prison.

That one was going to be fun!

"Grace, how's the image search coming?"

Her PA came over with her laptop.

"Not sure. I found a few stock photos of the Thames. But I'm still looking for something that says 'perfect village'. Don't know... what do you think of these?"

Sarah took a look. "That one," she said, pointing to a scene where the river curved by a mill and then wandered past a riverside restaurant. "It's not too bad."

"Still not spot on though, right?"

Grace had the same high standards she did, Sarah knew. Both of them wanted everything—image, layout, copy—to be as perfect as possible.

Sarah smiled and nodded.

"I'll keep digging."

"Good. I'm still playing with the navigation for the prison site. Creeping me out, it is."

Then a knock on the door, three strong raps.

Not often did they have customers come up the steps unannounced. Usually people called, discussed their needs, then a meeting was set up.

So this was unusual.

Grace opened the door and was faced with a bony-looking man in a herringbone three-piece suit, black umbrella tightly bound in hand, on this sunlit day.

He seemed to hesitate a moment, and then walked into the office as if it was his.

"The proprietor?" he said, with careful elocution.

"That would be me," Sarah said. "Can we help?"

The man shook his head, archly.

"*Au contraire*. It is I who can help *you*."

The man scanned the room and like a predator cornering some frail prey, saw a chair and went over to it.

"Do you mind?"

Not really a question at all.

Then he sat down and, from an inside pocket of his jacket, produced a business card and handed it to Sarah.

"Doctor Lawrence Sitwell," she read, "Professor of European

Archaeology, University of Oxford."

She noted—in much smaller letters—the initials *ret.*

As in 'retired'.

Sarah looked over to Grace who had stopped what she was doing to watch whatever was about to unfold with Lawrence Sitwell in this sunny office.

He produced a sheaf of papers from another pocket.

Sarah could see the logo of her newsletter—*Cherringham Roundel*—the distinctive arches of the medieval Cherringham Bridge across the Thames.

Interesting to see hard copy. Since it was an online newsletter, Sarah had only seen a print-out of the first two issues.

"I imagine it is you who wrote this... article?"

Clearly 'article' wasn't the word that he wanted to use.

"I do all of the writing. Except my assistant Grace sometimes—"

"This piece then—about the so-called discovery of the Roman plate and then—its theft—that is you?"

"Guilty," Sarah said.

This Sitwell chap—Sarah thought—*isn't sitting too well with me.*

"It is filled with errors of fact."

"That the plate was found? That it was stolen?"

Another dramatic roll of his head. The more agitated Sitwell became, the more his enunciation grew clipped, as if his mouth and teeth had turned into an old printing press, spitting out blocks of type into the air.

"The chances of that plate being genuine are virtually—nil. You can be absolutely sure that it is nothing more than another of those clap-trap replicas produced in the tens of thousands in the eighteen hundreds, and therefore absolutely worthless."

"Hang on, Professor."

"Your piece is just parroting a lot of ill-informed—"

Sarah leaned close.

This is my office, she thought. *And professor or not, this academic bully isn't going to run the show in the shop I built.*

"I said... *hang on.* Slow down. If you're here for a correction—"

"Correction?" he interrupted. "Dare say there should be more than that. Should be an investigation into this hoax, this... scam."

Sarah wondered if she should tell him that an investigation was in fact in progress.

And if he had information to add, the more the merrier.

"So you think the item, the plate was..."

"Worthless."

"But Professor Cartwright?"

And that was as if Sarah had just thrown a circuit breaker.

"Professor Peregrine Cartwright?" Sitwell produced a hearty 'ha' that filled the office. Sarah looked over to Grace who, for Sarah's benefit, produced a clown-like grimace at their fulminating guest.

"Old Peregrine's eyes are anything but falcon-like, Miss Edwards." Sitwell jutted a finger out, pointed at Sarah. "This is not the first time that he has jumped to conclusions."

"Oh really? I thought he was quite a respected—"

Sitwell shook his head dramatically, stopping her short.

"Respected! Hmph. His knowledge base of Roman metallurgy, well, I could write a whole paper on what he doesn't know. In fact, I *have.*"

"But Professor Sitwell, you yourself have not seen the object?"

"One of the men who found it took a photo at the site, you know that."

"But not terribly clear."

"Clear enough. Even covered in mud. A replica."

"So whoever stole it..."

Now Sitwell leaned close, for the first time a smile—albeit a creepy one—bloomed on his face.

"Exactly. They stole nothing. Petty theft at best."

Sarah shot another look at Grace.

Could be, she thought, *that Sitwell's right.*

And if so, not only were the police wasting their time, so were she and Jack.

But still, there was that key question…

"Someone did steal it, Professor. Along with other things of value belonging to Professor Cartwright."

"I am sure that any items of 'value' old Peregrine had squirreled away have long been sold. It's a little tough to make ends meet when your pension has been cut."

Sarah made a mental note to check up on exactly how Cartwright left Oxford.

Perhaps he hadn't been retired with full honours.

Sitwell seemed to freeze for a moment as if he had said something out of turn. But another snort, and he recovered his balance.

"There," Sitwell said, warming to his conclusion. "You have the unvarnished truth of this fiasco. I expect to see clarifying details in the next edition of this…" he waved the printout of the online newsletter.

"The *Roundel,*" Sarah said. "And I will certainly look into these things."

Sitwell stood up and sniffed the air, while gazing around the office.

Sarah stood as well. There was one more detail she wanted to ask him since he seemed to know so much about this affair.

"Professor Sitwell, before you leave."

Sitwell's eyebrows went up.

He must have been quite a sight in the classroom.

"Despite everything you have said, do you have any theories on who broke in and stole the plate?"

"Theories?"

At that, Sitwell laughed. Sarah couldn't imagine what she had asked that was so funny. "My 'theory' is that it would be someone who doesn't know a damn thing about Romano-British artefacts!"

Still chuckling, Sitwell turned, walked to the door and left the office.

Grinning, Grace said: "I wish we'd recorded that. Could have been Cherringham's first viral video."

Sarah laughed, wondering what his odd visit had meant. Was there something she and Jack were missing?

13.

JERRY CLUELESS

JACK HAD DECIDED that the pub, with an offer of a free pint or two would be the best inducement to get Jerry Pratt to meet him for a chat.

"Thanks for coming," Jack said as they both stood at the bar, waiting for their beers.

Jerry nodded, his eyes locked on Ellie pulling a pint of best bitter. Just after lunchtime, and young Jerry seemed mighty thirsty.

Taking the pint, foam spilling over the side, Jerry took a sudsy sip. "No problem, mate. Anything to get that damn treasure back."

"That's more the police's line," Jack said. "I'm just asking some questions. Helping out, as it were."

Another big gulp, suds giving way to beer.

"You're a Yank. Yanks are smart. Smarter than the local lot 'ere. Bleedin' keystone cops they are. Maybe with you helpin', we'll 'ave a better shot at finding them bastards who did this."

"Maybe."

Jack thought: *Yanks are smarter? Guy must watch too many American cop shows.*

"I was thinking it might help to hear your side of the story."

Jerry cocked an eyebrow, finally looking away from his beloved pint, suddenly wary.

"Yeah. My story? About how we found it?"

Jack shook his head. "No, the night of the break-in."

Jerry shook his head. "You seen us, didn't you? Celebrating right here. Even chatted with you. Me and Baz, both right here."

"I get that. Great celebration."

Jack looked around the quiet pub. The lunchtime rush was long over and the place was still in anticipation of the early afternoon crowd. "But after that, you went straight home?"

The question stopped Jerry.

Then a small grin.

"Not exactly, mate. Like I said—was a bit of celebration, and we—"

"You and Baz?"

Jerry nodded. "Yeah, we drove over to Boughton. Got ourselves a little…" Jerry lowered his voice, "massage."

"Really? You and Baz, hmm? That's not what Baz told me."

"Too right he didn't tell you. Poor sod's got a wife now, doesn't he? She hears about any goings on like that, and well—don't have to draw you a picture. Though must admit, he was none too steady once we got there."

"I can believe that. Looked like he had trouble holding his head up."

"That's not all he had trouble keeping up!" Jerry said, laughing loudly.

Jack didn't know what to believe - Baz's story of immediately crashing on the couch, or Jerry's little road trip for some stress relief. All things considered, the latter was more likely. He'd keep quiet though—none of his business, as long as it didn't impact the case.

Jack knew it would be easy to have the police check that the two

THICK AS THIEVES

of them did go to Boughton. Still, it didn't rule either of them out.

Jack nursed his beer, but when Jerry's emptied he gave a wave to Ellie for a refill.

"Thanks. Generous of yer."

"The next morning, you must have been really upset when that safe popped open?"

"Upset? Why I'd take whoever did that and—" Jerry caught himself.

Bit of a temper there.

"Understandable. Any thoughts on who could have done it?"

Jerry looked away.

"Dunno. Been told a thing like that is hard to fence."

"Almost impossible, is what I've learned."

"Right. So can't imagine any of us would have done it. We had a sure thing—"

He banged his glass down on the bar.

"Money in hand," he said.

Jack could feel the pain of all the cash vanishing overnight.

"So you think?"

"Must have been that gang the police are talking about. Hitting all the villages around here. Maybe they didn't even know it was there, won't know what the hell to do with it. I just know one thing,"

"What's that, Jerry?"

"Sure screwed up my life, know what I mean?"

Jack nodded, gave the bereft Jerry a smile.

"Think I do," he said.

Jack feigned looking at his watch.

"Gotta dash—thanks for talking though."

"Right. Anytime. And hope you find 'em, the ones that did it!"

Just a smile in response since—right now—that seemed pretty

unlikely, and Jack sailed out of the Ploughman's.

THICK AS THIEVES

14.

A DESPERATE LADY

TONY STANDISH LOOKED up at the grandfather clock that sat in the front corner of his office, next to two large windows that overlooked the High Street.

"She did say she'd be here at three o'clock sharp."

Sarah nodded. "Not to worry. I'm way ahead on deadlines for a change. I can wait."

Standish got up and walked to the floor-to-ceiling windows, and looked out.

The estimable Lady Repton had agreed to meet, but insisted it be at her solicitor's office, Tony Standish Esq—which was fine since Sarah trusted Tony implicitly.

Cherringham felt like a better place with a lawyer like Tony watching her back.

Funny though… she knew so little about his life, and he knew everything about hers, her parents, kids…

He looked down to the street, pulling aside the net curtain.

"Ah, there's her taxi. No driver, sadly. Those days are over."

He turned back to Sarah.

"Been a difficult time for her. Cutting back, and all that—"

"I can imagine."

Standish's receptionist knocked, and then opened the door to his office.

"Mr Standish, Lady Repton is here."

Tony nodded, keeping his position at the window, and then Lady Repton walked in.

Her cane punctuated every step with a sharp clack on the wood floor until she reached the thick plush Persian carpet, a crimson sea that surrounded Tony's desk and chairs for clients.

Lady Repton barely shot Sarah a nod as she made a surprisingly quick beeline for one of the chairs.

"Some tea, if you don't mind, Standish."

"Absolutely. Sarah?"

"I'm fine, Tony."

Repton snorted at that. Whether at Sarah's refusing a perfectly good cup of tea in the afternoon or calling *her* solicitor 'Tony', Sarah didn't know.

ONCE TEA HAD been brought in, Tony offered to take the lead starting the meeting.

"Lady Repton, as you know, Sarah, who is also a client, has been—"

"Oh, do get on with it. I'm not getting any younger, Standish. Let's cut to—what do the young people, say—the chase."

Lady Repton took a sip of the tea, both saucer and cup held perfectly, in a way they must have been drilled into young debutantes decades ago.

A century ago!

"Precisely. Sarah?"

Standish turned to Sarah, passing the ball.

Lady Repton kept her eyes locked, looking forward as Sarah

began.

"Lady Repton, I have been working with Mr Jack Brennan to see if we can learn anything about the plate that was stolen."

Repton shook her head in a move that screamed 'now I've heard everything'.

"Amateur detectives," Lady Repton said.

Another shake of her head.

Sarah was tempted to tell this woman that the two of them had had a good degree of success, and Jack was anything but an amateur. But she felt holding her tongue might better serve the cause here.

"I'd like to review with you the events of that morning."

Now the turret of Lady Repton's head turned, and with a slight angle adjustment, the lowering of her chin, she addressed Sarah squarely.

"The plate, worth a fortune, was *stolen*. Or did you not read your own pithy description of the event in that *thing* you publish."

"I know, Lady Repton. But did you notice anything else? Did anyone seem suspicious? Anyone there you think might have wanted to steal the plate?"

At that Lady Repton produced a loud 'ha'. "Maybe that dotty professor. I mean, it was his safe after all."

"But the police saw signs of the break-in. Other valuable things were stolen."

"Pish-posh. Right. And I have had it explained to me that the item is impossible to sell. Tremendous value, but if you are not dealing with the British Museum, virtually worthless."

"I've been told that as well."

And in that moment with Lady Repton's clear eyes locked on hers, Sarah realised that they both had the same thought.

Everyone is saying that it is impossible to sell. Nobody could buy it.

But was that true?

"Everyone there could have used that money so why steal it?"

Sarah took a deep breath before the next question.

A long pause, as she braced herself.

"And you too?"

Lady Repton had long perfected the art of the long, slow and deeply uncomfortable burn.

"Of course. Of course, I could have used that money." She looked around the room, avoiding eye contact. "No secret there. No end of things needed for the old estate. Lists a mile long. Hence," she looked back to Sarah. "I'm *not* pleased."

"I'm sure."

Sarah looked over to Standish who had forced a sheepish smile into place, his eyes seemingly suggesting that this little interview was over.

Sarah leaned forward and extended a hand.

"Thank you, Lady Repton, for coming here. Answering my questions. We will do what we can."

Lady Repton put her tea, half drunk, on the corner of Tony's deep mahogany desk.

Then the old battle-axe used the leverage of her cane to rise out of the classic wooden chair.

"I doubt that doing 'what you can' will mean anything. Still, I suppose I must wish you luck."

She took Sarah's hand in a surprisingly firm handshake.

"Now, Standish—a taxi, if you will?"

And like a prehistoric three-legged raptor, not to be underestimated, Lady Repton walked out the door.

15.

NO HEADWAY

JACK WATCHED CAREFULLY from the forward deck of the Grey Goose as Daniel loosened the rope, pulled it back into the little rowing boat and took hold of the oars. Riley the dog sat patiently in the stern, unperturbed as the tiny craft bobbed from side to side, next to the barge.

"Don't forget now, Daniel—take a good look up and down river."

Daniel checked like he was crossing the road for the first time.

Which in a sense he is, thought Jack.

"Tell me this gets easier," said Sarah standing next to Jack, anxiously watching her eleven-year old son row solo for the first time.

"Nope," said Jack. "I can guarantee you that when Daniel is twenty-one you will still be peering over his shoulder ready to pick him up when he falls. Or at the very least, pick up his rent bill when he phones home to say he's broke."

"All clear!" said Daniel.

"Well then… off you go, kid," said Jack.

Daniel dipped both oars in the water, pulled, and headed away across the river with Riley to the far bank. The water was flat calm and Jack noticed the insects skimming over the surface.

Maybe get the rods out later, catch myself some supper.

"Nearly there, Dan," called Sarah, a warning tone in her voice.

"He knows what he's doing," said Jack.

And sure enough, Jack could see Daniel check his distance from the bank, ship his oars and gently float to a perfect rest up against the little jetty. The boy looped his rope round the post, tied it off then jumped up onto the opposite bank. Riley leaped after him.

"Nice work Daniel," called Jack. "Give us a shout when you're ready to come back."

Daniel gave a big grin and a thumbs-up.

"Come on Riley!" he shouted, and raced off into the meadows. Riley tore after him.

Jack turned to Sarah.

"Kid's a natural," he said. "Couldn't have done it better myself."

"I seem to remember you use the outboard these days Jack."

"Gotta watch I don't put my back out."

"A likely story."

Jack winked at her then pulled out one of the canvas chairs that leaned against the table and sat down, facing the river. Daniel and Riley were already halfway across the meadows. Jack had a sudden and surprising pang of memory of being that age, his dog at his side, walking through waist-high grass.

Funny how an image like that can ambush you, he thought.

Sarah pulled out another chair and sat next to him.

"So you think there's nothing more we can do," she said, not taking her eyes off her son, fast becoming a dot in the distance.

Jack knew it was the case she was talking about.

They'd already spent the morning going round in circles—all the while planning for Jack's little party in a week's time. And though that was pretty organised, the investigation was going nowhere fast.

"Short of a surprise confession—nope," said Jack.

But he could see she still wasn't going to settle for that.

"I remember you told me once that when you get a breakthrough, it's often something that you knew already, but you just hadn't realised the importance."

"True," said Jack. "It's usually some fact or piece of information you've kind of... misfiled. You know what I mean?"

"Exactly," said Sarah. "So maybe you've got one of those now?"

Jack considered this.

"Well..."

"Go on."

"One thing I do not get," said Jack. "The break-in. They tried the front door, then they smashed the back door. Now from what you told me about this art gang from that crime report—they're pros. And anyone who can open one of those Canon safes—well they can slip a door lock easy."

"Plus—would they really smash the glass in and leave it there?"

"Exactly," said Jack.

Jack watched as a group of swans flew past, just level with the deck of the Grey Goose and landed downstream.

"On the other hand," he said. "The way Cartwright left the combination out, it might be an amateur who just got lucky."

"Like Jerry?"

"Not impossible. My money's on Lady Repton."

Sarah laughed.

"Can't be her. You'd have heard her cane tapping from here. What about young Baz?"

"Not on his own—he was too drunk. If local reports are to be believed."

"Pete the Farmer?"

"Possible—though I'd hate it to be true."

"Which leaves the professor," said Sarah.

"And with him, like we said before—where's the motive?"

"You're right," said Sarah. "Everybody says it would be impossible to sell the plate anyway. So whoever stole it might have just thrown it away."

"Or melted it down."

"But I wonder if that's really true?" said Sarah. "What about those people you hear about who have incredible works of art all hidden away? They exist, don't they? It's possible to buy these things on the black market."

"True," said Jack. "In fact, I remember, a year or two back there was a guy in the States bought a T-Rex skull for a small fortune. Texan oil millionaire. Had it installed in his study. Just to look at all on his lonesome."

"So the Cherringham Plate could still be out there."

"It could. But you know what? Right now, I don't think we're going to find it."

Across the river, Riley jumped up onto the bank and barked a greeting. Jack could see Daniel, stick in hand, heading back too.

"Not unless we get lucky," he said with a shrug. But from the determined look on Sarah's face, he could see she wasn't going to let it go that easily.

SARAH HAD JUST finished editing a blood-curdling scream into the Victorian Hangman Feature on the Penton Prison website when there was a knock at the office door.

She looked over at Grace.

"Are you expecting anyone?"

Grace shook her head and walked over to the door. Pete Butterworth entered quickly. He nodded a hurried greeting to Sarah and went straight to the little window that looked down onto the village square.

Sarah looked at Grace.

"What the…?" she mouthed.

Grace shrugged again.

"Mr Butterworth—is there a problem?" she said, standing up from her chair.

"No, not a problem," he said, not taking his eyes from the street two storeys below.

Sarah joined him at the window.

"You look worried."

"Worried? No."

For a second his eyes flicked away from the street to hers—then he pressed his face to the glass again.

"You see the BMW by the entrance to the village hall?"

Sarah looked down.

"The blue one, yes?"

"That's it," he said. "By the way—you can call me Pete."

"Nice to see you again, Pete."

"Hmm. Now don't take your eyes off the car—all right?"

"Absolutely. But are you going to tell me why?"

She saw Pete look over at Grace.

"Don't worry. Anything you were going to say to me, you can say in front of Grace."

He seemed to consider this for a few seconds, then relaxed.

"If you say so."

Sarah waited patiently.

"Go on then."

"Right. Well it's about the plate of course. The robbery."

Without taking his eyes off the street he launched into his story. And Sarah knew she and Jack were about to get lucky.

"Your friend—the American—when he came to the farm and spoke to me and Becky, well, I'm afraid we lied."

Pete looked away at this.

"He asked us what we did the night the robbery happened and we said we stayed in, went to bed early. But we didn't. Well—we did. At first. But I couldn't sleep. I was worried about the plate, you see. Worried that it wasn't safe at old Cartwright's place. So I got in the Land Rover and drove into the village. Parked out of the streetlights, just up from Cartwright's house. So I could keep an eye out, case anyone got ideas, know what I mean?"

Sarah knew exactly what he meant.

"In case Jerry and Baz decided to get the plate back?"

"Well. Yeah. Them—or worse still, some of their mates. I got a call from Billy down the Ploughman's—he told me they were in there shooting their mouths off, all but giving Cartwright's address away. So naturally—I got worried. We need that money, see. We need it so badly."

Sarah knew she also needed to keep the momentum going.

"So what time was that?"

"When I got there? I don't know, about one-ish. Two maybe. Anyway, I'd only been there half an hour when Jerry himself turns up. Half pissed I reckon. He did a kind of walk-by outside Cartwright's house, all inconspicuous—then he fell in the hedge."

"But he couldn't see you?"

"No, I was tucked down in the car. Anyway he opens the gate, goes to Cartwright's front door and tries to open it—with a credit card first. Then a screwdriver. Then he gives up, comes down the path, kicks the gate and heads off."

"So he didn't go round the back?"

"No. Definitely not. Anyway, soon as he's gone I'm thinking—I'd better get in there myself, get the plate, look after it, it's not safe. So I creep over and head up the path."

"You were going to steal it yourself?"

"No! Not steal it! Look after it. Stop them beggars from stealing it—"

"That's not the way the police would see it."

"Too right. Which is why I'm talking to you—okay? Anyway, that's not the important thing. It's what happened next. See, I'm halfway up the path when a light goes on round the back and there's a shadow, then I see somebody coming round the side of the house to the path."

"You got a proper look at them?"

"That's what I'm telling you. It was a bloke, thin scrawny bloke. And he was carrying a bag—like a sports bag—but heavy, like it had metal in it. Like it had the plate in it. He walks right past me down the path—I mean, I'm almost under his feet I'm so close, but I'm in the dark under a shrub, see—and as he goes I can see his face in the street light, dead clear. So, soon as he's out into the square I get up so I can follow him—but he's jumped in a car and he's gone. Gone with my plate."

"But you got a good look at him?"

"Oh yes."

"And you'd recognise him again?"

"Well I just did, didn't I? Why do you think I came up here? Why do you think we're looking at the BMW?"

Pete gestured with his head down to the car in the square.

Sarah realised—and followed his gaze, just as a man approached and from a distance unlocked the car with his keyfob.

"See—*that's* the bloke I saw coming out of Cartwright's house. That's the thief. I recognised him just now in the shop. I took his number—then came up here. You can trace him, find out who he is…"

As the man opened the car door, some instinct made him look up at the windows of Sarah's tiny office. She drew back, and felt Pete Butterworth pull back too, out of the light. And in that moment Sarah knew she wouldn't need to trace the car.

She'd seen the man before.

It was Lawrence Sitwell, one-time Professor of European Archaeology at the University of Oxford.

16.

UNDERCOVER

JACK POURED ANOTHER cup of tea from his metal flask and handed it to Sarah.

"That's the end of the tea," he said, draining the flask into his own mug. "And we had the last cookie an hour ago."

He leaned back into the front passenger seat of Sarah's Rav-4, yawned and looked around. The smart, tree-lined Oxford street was quiet. The first floor of number 23—Professor Sitwell's apartment—was dark, the curtains half-closed.

Late afternoon. What did academics do on spring afternoons?

Drink sherry and snooze till dinner, he thought.

"All we got left now is two dog biscuits I found in my pocket."

"Well, with luck we won't need those," said Sarah. "Because if the good professor doesn't emerge soon—we're going to have to head home so I can pick up Chloe from Drama Club."

"Sure wasn't like this in the old days," said Jack.

"In the old days you would have kicked the door down, dragged the suspect into the street and cuffed him."

"And you wouldn't?" ·

"Are you kidding?" said Sarah. "I can't imagine anything more fun."

Jack laughed.

"Even if he's not guilty?"

"Oh he's guilty all right."

"No need for a trial?" said Jack, smiling.

"Members of the jury—the accused was seen creeping out of the house in the middle of the night carrying a heavy bag…"

As she was talking, the heavy oak door of number 23 opened, and Sitwell emerged carrying a briefcase. The door slammed and he walked briskly towards them.

"Oh shoot," said Jack, spilling his tea and pulling out a map— any map—to read. Sarah pretended to lose something under the steering wheel and dropped her head out of sight.

Out of the corner of his eye, Jack saw Sitwell approach the car… and then stride past, heading towards the Banbury Road.

"Phew," he said, sitting up. "I thought he'd spotted us."

Sarah didn't answer—and then he realised it was because she was laughing too much.

"What's funny, huh? Look at my trousers. I got tea all over them."

Sarah wiped her eyes.

"Very professional, Jack. I can see I've got a lot to learn about surveillance."

Jack grunted. He didn't like looking stupid. But—he had to admit—he'd been too casual.

Need to sharpen up a bit if I'm going to do this kind of thing, he thought.

"Come on," he said. "We've still got an hour's parking left on the ticket. Let's see where he goes."

And, grabbing his coat from the back seat, he climbed out of the car, his eyes on the now distant figure of Lawrence Sitwell.

WITH SARAH TRACKING him on the other side of the road, the professor had been easy to follow.

Scurrying along, head down, Jack saw that Sitwell had the determined look of someone with an appointment to make—and he felt confident they wouldn't be spotted.

Jack had been to Oxford a couple of times before—once years ago with his wife Katherine, just before she'd died—but they'd only visited the centre, the colleges, the parks. These wide avenues, criss-crossed by tiny terraced streets, were a maze—but a fascinating one.

Sitwell clearly knew the area well, taking little short cuts, avoiding the students on bikes who flew by, a silent hazard. Jack and Sarah stayed a hundred yards behind, occasionally looking in shop windows, using other walkers as cover.

Eventually they hit a little street full of shops and bars—and a smart cafe into which Sitwell disappeared.

Jack waited in the doorway of a newsagents until Sarah joined him.

She had a woollen hat pulled down over her hair and he was sure Sitwell would never recognise her. Across the road they could see the academic being shown to a table for two in the window. The place was empty—and Jack realised it was too early for dinner and too late for lunch.

Afternoon tea, thought Jack. *How terribly quaint.*

"There's another cafe just a bit further down," said Sarah. "We can watch him from there."

"You sure?"

"Yes, it's a bit of a parents' hangout—but it serves the best cakes in Oxford," said Sarah. "No way am I walking down Walton Street without having one. I'll get us a table."

Jack watched her slip down the street then followed briskly

behind.

He pushed open the door of the cafe and breathed in the smell of fresh coffee.

Worth the trip just for that, he thought.

The place was bustling, crowded with mums and kids and buggies. Amazingly Sarah had found an empty table in the corner by the window. He joined her. It was perfect—Sitwell was clearly visible across the street, but they would be hidden by the angle of the window and the various theatre posters stuck all over it. Jack ordered a coffee and felt virtuous declining the offer of cake, though when Sarah's cake came he didn't reject the offer of a mouthful.

"So, what now detective?" said Sarah, licking her fingers.

He shrugged.

"I don't know, really," he said. "The whole point of this is just to get a sense of him. Who he is. What he does. Who he lives with—or not."

"So if he does have the plate, we can figure out where it might be?"

"Exactly," said Jack. "God, this coffee's good."

He kept his eyes on Sitwell, waiting impatiently at his table just across the road. The waiter had come over to him, but it looked like he'd declined to order—so Jack guessed he was waiting for someone to join him.

"You know, I should have suspected something was up when he came by to tell me the plate was worthless," said Sarah.

"Sounds like he's got some kind of grudge against Cartwright, too." As Jack watched, Sitwell pulled a laptop out of his briefcase and set it on the table.

"What I wouldn't give to know what he's up to on that thing," he said.

"Oh really?" said Sarah.

THICK AS THIEVES

She reached into her handbag and pulled out a tablet, flicked it on and swiped the screen a couple of times.

"How's your moral compass these days Jack?" she said, looking at him with a mischievous smile.

"Depends."

"Not much of a compass then."

"What are you asking me, Sarah?"

"What if I could tell you what he's 'up to' on that laptop?"

"You're kidding me."

"Couple of years ago, when my marriage unravelled, I er... acquired... a few extra computer skills. The sort of skills you need if you're going to hack into your cheating husband's email and web history and nail the lies that will remove him from your life for good."

"Ouch," said Jack. "Sounds like that still hurts."

"Oh, it does. Of course, when people ask me if I'm over it—I always say yes."

Jack hadn't taken his eyes off Sitwell, but he did now. He could see that Sarah was angry just recollecting those raw emotions.

"I guess that's why I've never asked you," he said. "I just assumed you wouldn't want to talk about it."

"And I appreciate that."

Jack nodded and looked back at Sitwell, tapping away at his computer.

"So. Let's be clear here. You can access that guy's laptop from this distance? On that?"

Sarah nodded.

"The cafe's got an open Wi-Fi network. I can see it. It's not encrypted. He's the only person in there right now—and I'd bet he's just logged on. I can get his sign-ins and passwords for pretty much everything he's doing. Without compromising any innocent bystanders."

"And you've got time to do it?"

"Are you kidding?" she said. "It'll take about two minutes, max."

Jack considered the situation and then laughed. "So what are you waiting for?"

Jack sipped his coffee while Sarah tapped away at the keyboard. After a minute she sat up straight, turned off the tablet and put it away in her handbag.

"Have you done it?" said Jack, surprised.

"Yep. I don't have time to check it out now. But when we get back home—and I've done tea for Chloe and Daniel—I'll let you know what I find."

"That easy huh?" said Jack. "No wonder kids are playing around inside the NSA and stealing secrets."

"You think what we just did is wrong?"

"Of course. But sometimes that's what you have to do."

"I don't make a habit of it, Jack. But in this case I feel sure enough he's involved to justify it."

Jack felt uncertain. He knew sometimes the end justified the means but this was different. Somehow... sneaky. He turned to look at Sarah again.

"Dangerous path," he said.

"I know."

"What if he's totally innocent?"

"He isn't."

"You sound pretty certain."

He could see that Sarah was smiling at him and he couldn't quite work out why.

"I am now," she said, nodding toward the cafe across the street. "Look who's just arrived."

Jack turned, just in time to see that someone had joined Sitwell at his table. The man had his back to them. He gave the professor an affectionate hug and the briefest of kisses on one cheek, before pulling out a chair and sitting down.

Then, as he turned to call the waiter, his face was clearly visible.

It was Professor Peregrine Cartwright.

"Well, how about that," said Jack.

17.

A CUNNING PLAN

SARAH GOT TO the office by six—the sun had only just risen as she parked in the square and the streets of Cherringham were totally deserted.

She was early for two reasons. Firstly, she wanted to access Lawrence Sitwell's online life while he was most likely still asleep— just in case he tried to log in too and realised he'd been hacked.

And secondly, she didn't want Grace to be in the office while she did it. Grace had signed up to be an assistant in a web design agency—not become sidekick to a hacker with no regard for the law.

Although she'd been hoping to give Jack the results of their little adventure to Oxford the night before, by the time she'd picked up Chloe, cooked the kids' dinner, helped with homework and put a wash on it was eleven o'clock and she was exhausted.

So she'd rung Jack and told him to drop by the office in the morning—and then fallen fast asleep.

She'd woken up on the sofa at two in the morning, with the lights still on and dragged herself off to bed.

Now, with the sun streaming in, a pot of coffee brewing in the office kitchen, her headphones on and her favourite playlist running, she knew she could really make some progress.

She pulled her chair up to the main computer, copied the user names and passwords from her tablet, and started to explore the virtual world of the eminent Professor Lawrence Sitwell…

JACK LEANED IN and tapped the side of the computer screen and Sarah jumped back in her seat in surprise.

"Didn't meant to frighten you—but I've been saying 'hi' for the last couple of minutes. You'll damage your ears playing it that loud you know."

"Morning, Jack," she said, taking off her headphones, grinning. "That's what I tell my kids."

Jack handed her a fresh cup of coffee and she took it gratefully.

"What time is it anyway?"

"Nearly nine," said Jack. "What you got?"

"A lot," she said.

"Well, let's hear it."

"Okay," she said, quickly assembling her thoughts into some kind of order. "Professor Sitwell retired. And Professor Cartwright retired. Coincidence? No. The two of them have been colleagues for the last ten years or so, working in the same field."

"So Sitwell's attack on Cartwright is just a sham, huh?"

Sarah nodded.

"On the surface, they cultivate a kind of professional rivalry—each one publishing a book that rides on the back of the other, critiques it, moves the ideas on. But really they're not rivals. They've been partners all that time."

"Partners in crime too, huh?"

"Definitely. It seems both of them took early retirement two years ago after certain 'irregularities' were discovered in the finances of a charity they were involved in."

"What kind of charity?"

"It was set up to rescue ancient artefacts from war-torn Middle Eastern states."

"Very convenient."

"Exactly," said Sarah. "When the Charities Commission began to make noises, the University got worried that they might be drawn into some kind of scandal, so our two professors were 'invited' to leave—without a pension it seems."

"No criminal charges?"

"The police never got involved. I've got email threads going back to the beginning. They started off pleading their innocence. Then they said it was all a mistake. Then in the end they owned up to 'diverting' some funds—but only 'to save great pieces for mankind'.

"You believe that?" said Jack.

"The university clearly didn't. But they did agree to hush the whole thing up. Which was foolish really."

"Why?"

"Because—as I have found from exploring various websites that Professor Sitwell has signed up to—he and Cartwright have been pretty active in selling those same artefacts for cash. To support their own project."

"Let me guess—that project is their retirement?"

"Yep, for the last year, the two professors have also been sharing details of Greek villas for sale. Six bedrooms, swimming pool, private jetty, olive trees, vineyards—you know the kind of thing?"

"Of course, even with the crash—Greek villas don't come cheap."

"Exactly," said Sarah. "Which is why the Cherringham Plate must have been so tempting."

"Irresistible. So when Pete Butterworth saw Sitwell leaving the house, he hadn't broken in—he'd popped round to take the plate off Cartwright's hands for safe-keeping."

"The two of them must have come up with the plan together," said Sarah. "I suspect they did it by text and phone mostly—but there are enough emails here to prove pretty conclusively that they stole the plate themselves."

"And they smashed the window at the back?"

"Exactly—and Sitwell left with a random assortment of Cartwright's coins and miniatures."

"Just enough to make it look like a genuine theft," said Jack.

"The big surprise for them both was the damage to the front door. They're still emailing each other about that, wondering who did it."

"Poor old Jerry," said Jack, shaking his head. "If he hadn't tried to break in, the police might have been more suspicious of the back door damage."

"They couldn't believe their luck when the investigation pointed at the art gang. In fact, they're still gloating about it. Not for long though."

"What do you mean?" said Jack.

"Well—we've bust them wide open, haven't we?" said Sarah. "All we need to do now is pass on the emails to the police—and Alan gets his arrests."

"As if."

Sarah felt confused—all this work—it was a rock solid case, wasn't it?

"What do you mean?"

"Sarah—that's the very last thing we can do."

Jack stood up, went to the office door and pressed it gently shut.

"If you show this stuff to the police, it won't be them that gets arrested—it'll be you."

"Oh."

"And even if they didn't arrest you—not only would they not be able to use it in court they wouldn't even be able to look at it themselves. It's been illegally obtained—it's completely inadmissible."

"But that's crazy!" said Sarah. "They're guilty. They stole the plate."

"You know that. I know that. But we can't tell anyone else."

Sarah sat back in her chair exhausted and frustrated. All of yesterday, all of the morning so far—a total waste of time.

"You know—right now—Lawrence Sitwell is logging onto sites that traffic in artefacts and telling the whole world he's got something very interesting to sell. And we can't touch him?"

"Nope."

She took a deep breath and got up, went over to the window and looked down into the square. The shops were open. In the village hall opposite, the Tuesday Pilates class had got underway. People were going to work, going to school.

And just across the square, Peregrine Cartwright—she was sure of it—sat drinking his morning tea, reading *The Times*, eating bacon and eggs, utterly unconcerned that he was depriving Pete Butterworth, Jerry, Baz, Lady Repton and Cherringham itself of the just rewards of their extraordinary find.

She felt angry. No, *furious*.

She wanted to go downstairs, cross the square, bang on Cartwright's door, grab his cooked breakfast and shove it in his flabby, pompous face.

And then she thought of a much better solution.

She turned from the window, suddenly filled with excitement.

"How's your Texan, Jack?"

18.

LOVELY BOATING WEATHER

JACK ADJUSTED HIS silk cravat and opened one more button on his pressed pink cotton shirt. His face itched from the beard and moustache which Sarah had spent an hour gluing on that morning. With that, a Stetson and a false tan he was beginning to wish he'd never agreed to the crazy idea.

"I'm not so sure about this, Sarah. Looks to me more like something out of Jeeves and Wooster than Houston Texas."

Sarah handed him one of his long cigars.

"If in doubt—stick a cigar in your mouth Jack and think of Dallas."

"Hmm. I missed the re-runs of that show so you'll have to forgive the accent."

"Make it up. You think these guys know a real Texan from a Manhattan cop?"

"Let's hope not."

"Besides—don't forget that they *want* you to be true."

He turned from the mirror in the yacht's cabin to inspect the rest of his crew.

Sarah's father, Michael, was dressed in impeccable whites, with a captain's cap.

"Ready when you are, Mr Fielding sir," said Michael with a big grin.

He's loving this, thought Jack. *Guess it's like being back in action.*

Grace—Sarah's assistant—had a smart little black dress, and looked the part of the perfect PA.

"I've got the pre-lunch drinks chilling up in the top deck cooler, and the starters all prepped to serve once we get under way, Jack," she said. "Oops—I mean Mr Fielding sir! Sorry sir!"

Jack laughed—Grace was going to pull this off brilliantly and he knew whatever happened he'd be able to rely on her.

Only Sarah wasn't dressed up in disguise—but then if everything went according to her plan, she wouldn't be appearing till it was all over.

"You got everything set up?" he said.

"I've got a digital recorder up top which can store a day's worth of recording, plus our own Wi-Fi network."

"And my little cover story?"

"Any time you want to show the guys your 'lil place back home' I've got your Facebook page lined up with photos of the mansion, the horses, the pretty wife, the two beautiful kids at Harvard, the private jet…"

"Missing it already," said Jack. "How we doing on time?"

"Curtain up in ten—if they're on time."

"Well, I guess we should take our places for the opening number," said Jack. "All on top who are going on top…"

JACK SAT BACK in the plump, white leather armchair on the deck of the Mercury 80 'executive yacht' and surveyed the scene.

They were moored on a beautiful tree-lined stretch of the Thames, just up from the centre of Oxford. Other day boats and houseboats were moored alongside them—but the brilliant white sweeping lines of the Mercury screamed ostentatious, spare-no-expense wealth.

The perfect boat for visiting Texan oil millionaire, Osgood Fielding, a man with unlimited cash to spend on Roman treasure and a shared desire to keep the deal out of sight of the authorities.

Jack had been surprised how quickly the scam had fallen into place—but then Sarah was not only one hell of a hard worker, but she knew her way around all things digital.

Within a few hours she'd created an online identity for Jack as a prodigious buyer of artefacts on some of the dark sites that Sitwell and Cartwright frequented.

And within a day of his first posts going out onto message boards—under the pseudonym '*Croesus*', announcing that he was in the UK looking for 'unique pieces'—he'd been pinged by the professors suggesting a meeting to discuss a 'business proposition'.

Sarah had come up with the idea of the yacht. Her father had borrowed one—*The Emerald Princess*—from a friend in the village—'one of those gin palaces you love to hate, Jack'. And Grace had begged to play a role in 'taking that Sitwell bloke down a peg or two'.

All of which had led them here to Oxford. They'd motored downriver to the City at dawn, sorted Jack's disguise, taken in supplies for an extravagant lunch on the way…

Lobster and champagne, I can hardly wait, he thought.

… then promised the two academics a leisurely cruise and the possibility of an exchange—in cash—at the end of it, if the 'unique artefact' passed muster.

The bait had been set—and the greedy professors had taken it.

And here they are, bang on time, thought Jack.

For just downriver, he could see two familiar figures crossing over the little iron bridge that led from the City towards their mooring.

They were carrying a bag. And Jack could see it was heavy.

He called gently down into the well of the boat, "It's showtime folks. Better get into position. And don't forget—I'm Mr Osgood Fielding and I am made of more money than I know what to do with."

"Break a leg," called Sarah gently from down in one of the cabins.

Jack laughed to himself.

Boy, was he going to enjoy this.

Taking Professor Lawrence Sitwell (retired) and Professor Peregrine Cartwright (retired) for the ride of their lives...

JACK STOOD UP, champagne glass in hand as the two professors walked up the gangplank onto *The Emerald Princess*.

Far cry from the Grey Goose, Jack thought.

This yacht probably could handle a stormy North Sea without a problem.

Cartwright looked to be taking it all in as he spotted Jack, in his Stetson, waiting.

"Permission to come aboard?" he said gleefully.

Sitwell, holding the bag with—Jack hoped—the plate, seemed in a grimmer mood, eyes scanning left and right.

With perfect timing, Grace appeared carrying a silver tray with two flutes of bubbly.

"Hell, ya," Jack said (and immediately reminded himself not to overplay the Texas thing). "Welcome aboard, gents."

The two men, much shorter than Jack, stood side by side, each taking the offered champagne.

Jack kept his sunglasses on—the bright sun making this a near perfect day for a gentle roll upstream.

"You fellas hungry? Had chef prepare a bunch of things. Makes the damndest little lobster rolls. And his cheese puffs? I eat 'em like popcorn."

The men smiled, maybe feeling they had wandered onto the site of an unbelievable overly-American TV show.

Big Jack and his Billions.

"Yes," Sitwell said. "Sounds delightful."

Jack clapped the stiff Sitwell on the back. "Great. And weather's nice enough that we can sit on the aft deck. Transact our little…" and here Jack leaned close, voice conspiratorial, "business."

He led the way as—on cue—Sarah's dad Michael appeared above them on the bridge, in dress whites and captain's cap.

"Cap'n, you can get us under way *pronto.*"

"Yes, sir," Michael said with a crisp salute, crisp enough that it almost made Jack laugh.

Think we're all enjoying this way too much, he thought.

The regular crew of the boat had been asked to actually get the boat under way. All Michael had to do was play the role.

Jack indicated a trio of classic deck chairs at the back, each with a wooden side table to hold drinks and snacks.

"Okay, Professors, just—"

Sitwell looked around, raised a hand. "We prefer that you not address us as such. One can't be too careful."

Another clap on the back, Jack getting it. "Right. Gotcha."

Jack killed his champagne, and Grace appeared with a tray.

"Would you care for another, Mr Fielding?"

"How about something stronger, Grace. Some bourbon, neat? Gents?"

The two men sat down, shaking their heads, obviously nursing their champagne. Grace went away.

The *Emerald Princess* began moving up the river, slowly, steadily and Jack sat back in his chair, the brim of his Stetson down.

"So, how about we begin the ne-go-tia-tions, hmm?"

The men looked at each other, and Jack noted that Stilwell's hand hadn't released the bag.

BUT QUICK DISCUSSIONS weren't on offer, so Jack had lunch served as the boat glided upriver past open meadows, woods and small villages and under stone bridges.

Sitwell was sharp enough to ask 'Osgood' about his collecting practices and areas of interest.

Jack had rehearsed particulars, such as the opportunities that Middle East turmoil created for 'entrepreneurs' like him.

He finished the bourbon—which was really a few fingers of dark tea.

"But I always knew that there are prizes right *here*. Just damned hard to get at. Know what I mean?"

Cartwright was all too eager to agree. "Oh, we do. The

law is so very strict."

Now Jack looked around as if concerned that the ship's walls might have ears. "Yeah, damndest law." He slapped Cartwright on the knee. "Whatever happened to finders-goddamned-keepers?"

"Yes," Cartwright said, head bobbing.

The boat meanwhile had picked up a bit of speed. Not that either of the two men noticed.

Sitwell—sniffed, cleared his throat.

"Perhaps we should discuss terms?"

"Terms?" Jack shook his head, grinning. "You mean how much I'm going to pay you fellas for this contraband?"

"Finders… keepers?" Sitwell said.

"Too-shay!" Jack said. "I like you two. Marchin' to the beat of your own drummer. Right now," Jack's voice shifted, suddenly serious. And, he hoped, a bit intimidating. "I need to see the item, friends. I'm assuming that since you're prof—um *people* who know things, that I have no concern about authenticity, correct?"

"None whatsoever," Cartwright pronounced. Then he turned to Sitwell, who with a dramatic flair hefted the leather bag onto his lap, unzipped it, and pulled out the oversized plate.

And, now cleaned up by the two men, the plate was indeed a stunning item to see, the silver glistening in the sun.

No wonder people would pay millions for such things.

"Nice," Jack said. "A real beauty. Gonna look mighty sweet on my mantel on the ranch in Houston."

Sitwell nodded.

"May I?" Jack said, extending his hands. And as if passing something immensely fragile, Sitwell gave the plate to Jack, who took it and held it up to the sun.

Jack ran his fingers across the intricate silverwork. Satyrs dancing, sea-nymphs and Roman gods, some of which Jack recognised—Bacchus, Pan, Hercules…

He saw Cartwright scan the river bank, maybe worried that someone would see it, know what was happening here.

But this part of the river was quiet, secluded. Then the professor peered at him.

"I wonder, Mr Fielding—have we met before?"

"Hell no—you think I'd ever forget meeting a famous archaeologist like you?" said Jack slapping him on the thigh.

"We're getting rather close to Cherringham," Sitwell said, not hiding the nervousness in his voice.

"Are we? Not a place I ever heard of."

Jack saw the two men share a nervous glance and he knew he had to distract them.

"How about one point five million US dollars?"

And for a second nobody said anything.

19.

MONEY IN THE BANK

"WE WERE HOPING," Cartwright said, "for——"

"The figure discussed," Sitwell said, "was two million. That was the agreed sum."

Jack nodded, sat back in his chair, all smiles gone. "True enough, gents. But y'see, we are talking about an illegal item right here, aren't we? We're not in the Hindu Kush where anything goes. No siree. And I would still have to get this beauty out of the country."

Sitwell did not look pleased.

But Jack knew that being a tough negotiator was part of this deal.

"Tell you what. You two seem like nice fellas." Now a laugh. "Hate to disappoint you. So how about one point seven five?"

Nothing then—save for the sound of the mammoth *Princess*'s engine just below them.

Cartwright looked at Sitwell. Sitwell looked at Cartwright.

Their eyes carrying out a form of non-verbal communication.

Then they turned and—in unison—said, "Yes."

Jack slapped his knee as if he had just leaped off a bucking bronco.

Then he grabbed their hands, shaking both at the same time, nearly rattling them off their deck chairs.

"That's great, gents. Great!"

The *Princess* had picked up even more speed. Jack stood up.

A signal to Michael which would then be passed on to Sarah.

"And the funds?" Sitwell said.

"No problemo, Professor."

Jack pointedly ignored the previous injunction to avoid tell-tale titles.

"Pass me your bank details. Bank of Cyprus, yes?"

Sitwell nodded.

"I'll go, get that cash transferred—a-sap, as they say. You two sit here, enjoy the sun. Have another lobster roll—damn good, right?"

Jacks started towards the middeck and the cabin where Sarah waited.

"Be back in a jiff."

"HOW'D IT GO?" Sarah said.

She heard Jack's voice as it returned to normal. What she had overheard of his Texan had been so thick.

"Think I overplayed it, but they seemed to enjoy it. Here's the bank info. Sure you can do this?"

Sarah sat with her laptop open, ready to use Sitwell's hacked information to make it look like the massive deposit had hit his account.

"It will look completely real, Jack. Wi-Fi is a bit sketchy here. But still."

She took the bank account information. She could create a false memo, showing the transfer, and then send a secure email to Sitwell.

She had known that they would use the Cyprus bank, far enough away that the transfer might go unnoticed, and it was no doubt perfect for their dream of sunny isles and ouzo.

All about to disappear.

"Okay, think it's set."

She scanned it. The account number and bank transfer information looked perfect. The figure was staggering.

She looked up at Jack. "Almost feel sorry for them."

"Ill-gotten gains," Jack said. "But you're right, it is a bit sad, hmm?"

"But not *that* sad. Hitting *send*."

And in a flash the email was flying to Sitwell's mailbox, confirming the life-changing transfer.

"You called Alan?"

"Done," said Sarah. "Time for the last act, 'Osgood'."

Jack laughed. "What a name." And he put his Stetson back on and hurried to the aft deck, the *Princess* moving at a fast clip.

"WE ARE MOVING faster, Mr Fielding, aren't we?"

Jack looked around as if confused by the question.

"Dunno. I leave the captaining to the captain. But think we're just about done here. Want to see if you got confirmation? The eagles should have landed by now."

Sitwell dug out his smart phone while Cartwright pulled his chair close, looking at the small screen as if it was a genie's lamp.

Sitwell's voice was reverential. "It's there."

"Oooh!" Cartwright said.

Jack sat back on the chair. Bait taken. Cherringham just minutes ahead.

"Now, if you don't mind—"

Sitwell nodded eagerly, and passed the leather satchel to Jack.

Jack knew that Michael was watching from above. He smiled and took the satchel, a quick unzip to make sure that the item was still there.

He slowly removed his Stetson, the sunglasses, the false beard and moustache.

Then in the street-worn voice of a NY detective, Texan Osgood Fielding vanished.

"Gentlemen, welcome to... Cherringham."

And as the *Princess* kept a steady pace, other engines, and then sirens, filled the air.

A pair of fast-moving RIBs appeared from just behind a bend on the river. Down at that bend, a trio of police cars sat, lights flashing.

Sarah came running out of her cabin.

Sitwell and Cartwright stood up.

"You? What are *you* doing here?" asked Sitwell, though he'd clearly just put it all together.

"Making sure that you did not get one point seven five million dollars."

The *Princess* slowed, her crew lowering a stairway for the arriving officers in their RIBs.

Very smooth, Jack thought. In the first group of cops he could see Sarah's pal Alan—exactly as they'd planned.

Then Sitwell, eyes wide, trapped and panicky, did something that was—to Jack—unexpected.

He grabbed the leather bag that Jack had put on the floor, ran to the railing of the yacht and leaped overboard.

Cartwright remained frozen—even as Jack and Sarah watched Sitwell sink like a stone.

Jack turned to Sarah. "That's one heavy plate. Would have thought he knew that. I mean, being a professor and all."

Sarah laughed. "Maybe he never studied buoyancy."

Meanwhile from the nearest boat, Jack watched Alan peel off his vest, kick off his shoes and dive into what must be a chilly Thames.

"Go Alan," Jack called out.

The Cherringham police officer surfaced with a gasping Sitwell held in the rescue position as Alan swam to the shore.

"The pl-plate!" Sitwell said, sputtering.

"Be funny if they couldn't find it. Lost treasure... lost again," Sarah said.

Jack turned to her.

"I think they'll find it. And a lot of people's lives will change because of it."

Sarah nodded. "I'm rooting for Pete and Becky."

"Me, too," Jack said as officers, now aboard, cuffed Cartwright who was acting as though he'd got off at the wrong train station.

And as they dragged him away, Alan got to the shore with Sitwell, the collar his.

Then Jack turned to Sarah. "After this, hosting the party—"

"It'll be a piece of cake."

A DROP-IN ON THE GOOSE

ALAN, IN CIVILIAN clothes, stood close by Sarah, a glass of wine in his hand.

"Nice party," he said.

"Isn't it?" Sarah said, looking around the interior of Jack's boat.

Most of the people who came—which was a good number of the village—stayed for much longer than what a 'drop-in' would call for.

Not only did they all seem to enjoy spending some time on the barge on what turned out to be an uncommonly warm day, they also relished talking to people they saw every day, but normally only smiled and nodded to.

That was interesting, thought Sarah.

She saw Jack talking to dear Tony Standish who had arrived early, and, hours later, was still here.

Her mum and dad had insisted on manning the clean-up… and empty plates and finished glasses were quickly scooped up.

Even Daniel and Chloe wanted to come, and they dived in, replacing crackers and snacks while charming everyone.

She saw Jack look over and smile. And she smiled back, as if to say… *we've done good*.

"You know," Alan said, "I've started getting used to the two of you being of some help."

Sarah turned back to him.

Though Alan could be a by-the book person, even rigid, today he seemed looser, relaxed.

People can change, she thought.

"Thanks Alan—but you know it took you diving into the water to recover Sitwell and the plate."

Alan grinned at the memory. "Diver training. Search and recovery. All basic skills. But seriously—though I'm not saying you should just do what you want—this 'trick' of yours has been a great help."

Jack walked over with Tony.

"I am afraid Sarah, I must go," Tony said. "Need to visit Mum who you know would have loved to be here as well."

Alan looked at his watch.

It was a good forty minutes after the party was supposed to have ended and the sun was going down; the golden glow fading from the deck and the interior of the Grey Goose.

"But smashing party, Jack! Absolutely smashing!"

Sarah looked outside. A few of the other guests—Hope, Grace, and even Lady Repton who seemed to be lecturing the vicar—had walked down the gangplank but seemed reluctant to leave, still chatting on shore.

Yes, she thought, *this has been a very special event.*

Tony turned to Jack, and put a hand on the former NYC detective. "Jack—I think you should do this every year!"

Jack grinned, looked at Sarah.

"Agreed. Put it on your calendar."

"Terrific!" Tony said.

It gave Sarah enormous pleasure to see Jack saying goodbye to his guests, and feeling like he was fitting in. No—more than that.

And then the last guest, Jerry Pratt turned around to discover that the party had in fact ended and, with a sheepish grin, sailed out wobbly to the deck, onto the gangway and the safety of the shore.

And the party was over.

WHILE HER PARENTS and kids tackled the washing-up, Sarah spotted Jack out on the deck, enjoying a massive cigar as he watched the last guests make their way back to the village.

When he saw her, he turned, rolling the cigar between thumb and finger.

"Great party, hmm?" he said.

She nodded. But then:

"You know, Jack, it was more than a great party."

He took a puff and tilted his head.

"What do you mean?"

"Seeing everyone today, all these locals mixed up, laughing, talking—it wasn't something you normally see here."

"Class thing or something?"

"Maybe. But I think all of them are seeing themselves through your eyes, seeing each other as if *they* had arrived in this village."

"Interesting. Fresh eyes?"

"More than that," said Sarah looking over to the fields, already rich with the grasses and shrubs roaring back to life.

She took a breath. "It's that you've grown to love Cherringham, that you love the pubs, the fields—"

"This river."

A smile "Yes. I think it's made them appreciate their world all the more."

"Really?" Another puff. "Well, I have to tell you one thing."

"Yes?"

"If I've given something back to the village, it doesn't compare…"

His voice lowered, and she thought for a moment that he might even choke up.

"… does not compare, to what it's given me."

At which point her father and mother appeared, Michael holding a tray with four cut-crystal glasses, each with a half inch of dark liquid at the bottom.

"Sixteen-year-old Lagavulin," Michael said. "A toast?"

"Absolutely," Jack said.

He held up the glass.

"To Cherringham."

Answered by clinking, then all their voices, loudly…

"To Cherringham!"

NEXT IN THE SERIES:

CHERRINGHAM

A COSY CRIME SERIES

LAST TRAIN TO LONDON

Matthew Costello & Neil Richards

Cherringham is devastated. Otto Brendl, the likeable old man who hosted the classic Punch-and-Judy show for the kids each summer, has died suddenly of a heart attack. But while the memorial service is being planned, Jack becomes suspicious that maybe there's more behind the heart attack?

Soon Jack and Sarah are on the trail of a particularly sinister murderer—and together they will realise that there's more than one kind of justice.

ABOUT THE AUTHORS

Matthew Costello (US-based) and **Neil Richards** (UK) have been writing TV scripts together for more than twenty years. The best-selling Cherringham series is their first collaboration as fiction writers: since its first publication as ebooks and audiobooks the series has sold over a million copies.

Matthew is the author of many successful novels, including *Vacation* (2011), *Home* (2014) and *Beneath Still Waters* (1989), which was adapted by Lionsgate as a major motion picture. He has written for The Disney Channel, BBC, SyFy and has also written dozens of bestselling games including the critically acclaimed *The 7th Guest*, *Doom 3*, *Rage* and *Pirates of the Caribbean*.

Neil has worked as a producer and writer in TV and film, creating scripts for BBC, Disney, and Channel 4, and earning numerous Bafta nominations along the way. He's also written script and story for over 20 video games including *The Da Vinci Code* and *Broken Sword*.

Printed in Great Britain
by Amazon